Dear parents, caregivers, and educators:

If you want to get your child excited about reading, you've come to the right place! Ready-to-Read *GRAPHICS* is the perfect launchpad for emerging graphic novel readers.

All Ready-to-Read *GRAPHICS* books include the following:

★ **A how-to guide to reading graphic novels for first-time readers**

★ **Easy-to-follow panels to support reading comprehension**

★ **Accessible vocabulary to build your child's reading confidence**

★ **Compelling stories that star your child's favorite characters**

★ **Fresh, engaging illustrations that provide context and promote visual literacy**

Wherever your child may be on their reading journey, Ready-to-Read *GRAPHICS* will make them giggle, gasp, and want to keep reading more.

Blast off on this starry adventure . . . a universe of graphic novel reading awaits!

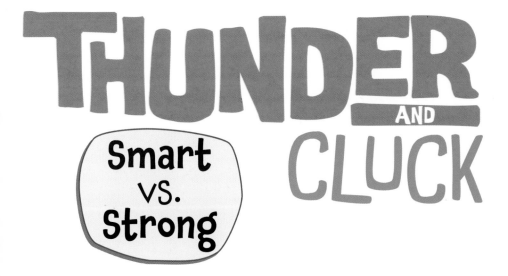

THUNDER AND CLUCK

Smart vs. Strong

For Leo & Hallie
—J. E.

For every teacher—T. REX HUGS!
—M. T.

SIMON SPOTLIGHT
An imprint of Simon & Schuster Children's Publishing Division
1230 Avenue of the Americas, New York, New York 10020
This Simon Spotlight edition December 2021
Text copyright © 2021 by Jill Esbaum
Illustrations copyright © 2021 by Christopher M. Thompson
All rights reserved, including the right of reproduction in whole or in part in any form.
SIMON SPOTLIGHT, READY-TO-READ, and colophon are registered trademarks
of Simon & Schuster, Inc. For information about special discounts for bulk
purchases, please contact Simon & Schuster Special Sales at 1-866-506-1949 or
business@simonandschuster.com.
Manufactured in the United States of America 1021 LAK
10 9 8 7 6 5 4 3 2 1
This book has been cataloged with the Library of Congress.
ISBN 9781534486584 (hc)
ISBN 9781534486577 (pbk)
ISBN 9781534486591 (ebook)

THUNDER AND CLUCK

Smart vs. Strong

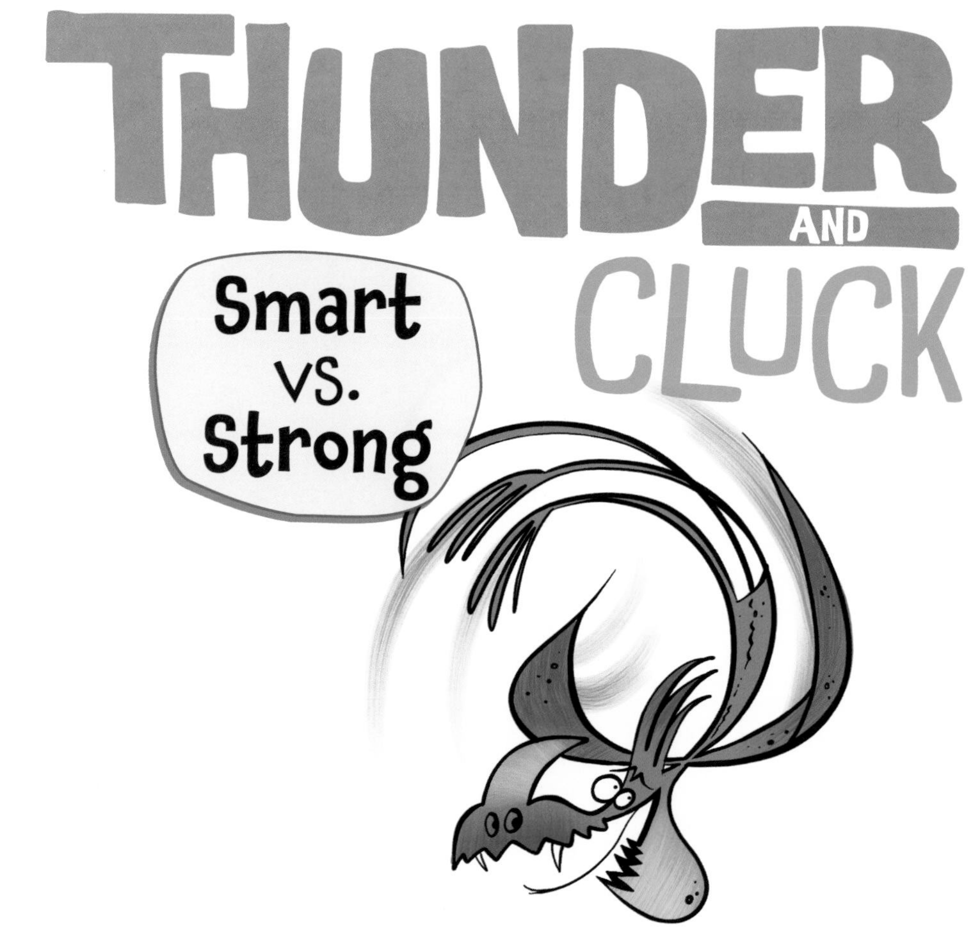

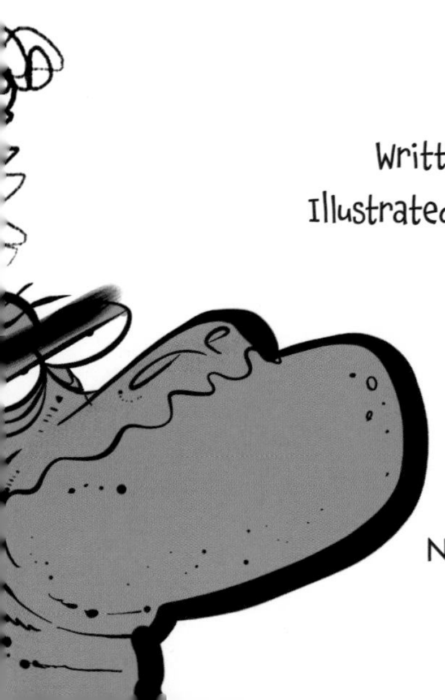

Written by JILL ESBAUM
Illustrated by MILES THOMPSON

Ready-to-Read *GRAPHICS*

Simon Spotlight
New York London Toronto Sydney New Delhi

HOW TO READ THIS BOOK

THUNDER and CLUCK are here to give you some tips on reading this book.

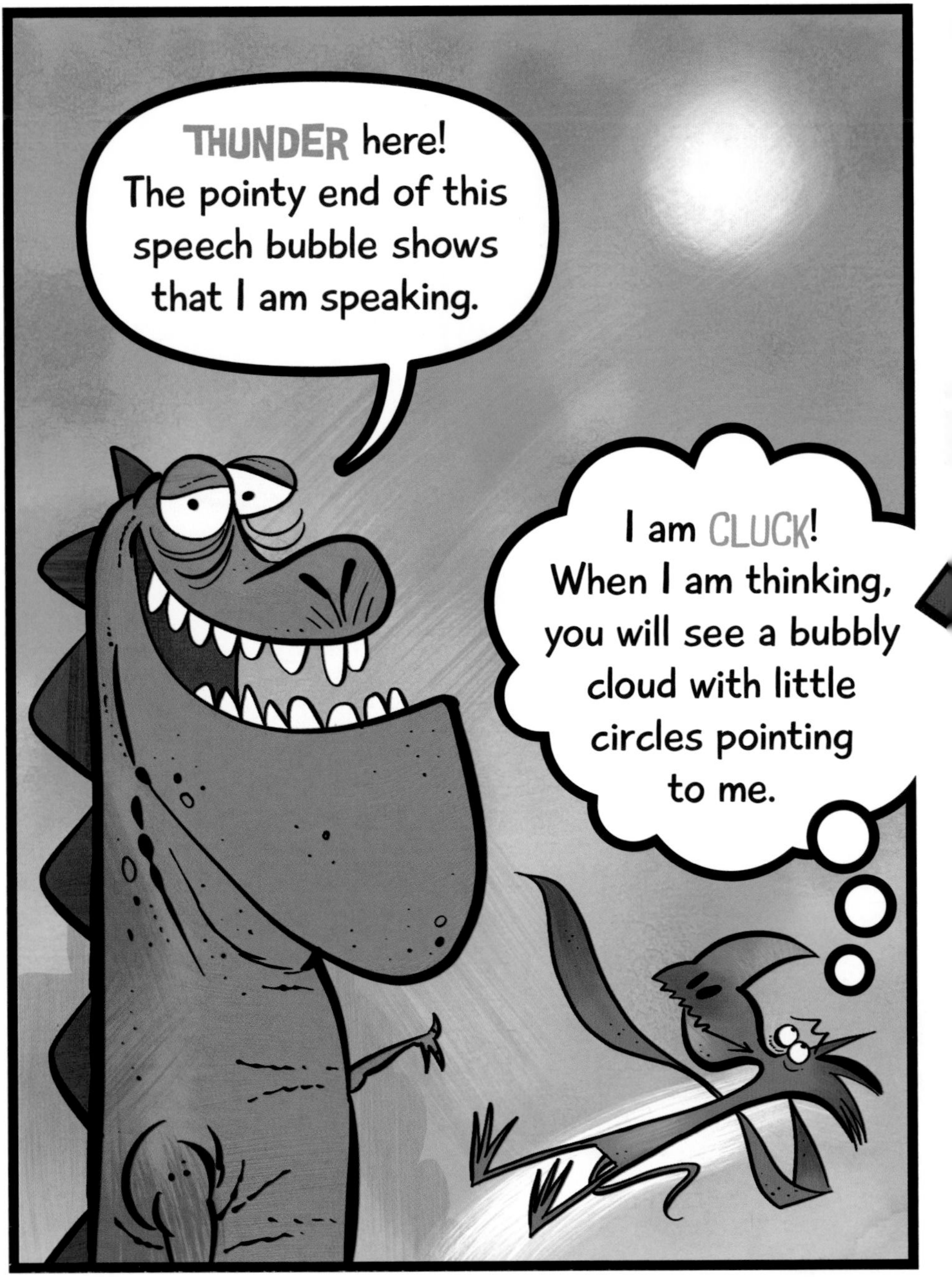
THUNDER here! The pointy end of this speech bubble shows that I am speaking.
I am CLUCK! When I am thinking, you will see a bubbly cloud with little circles pointing to me.

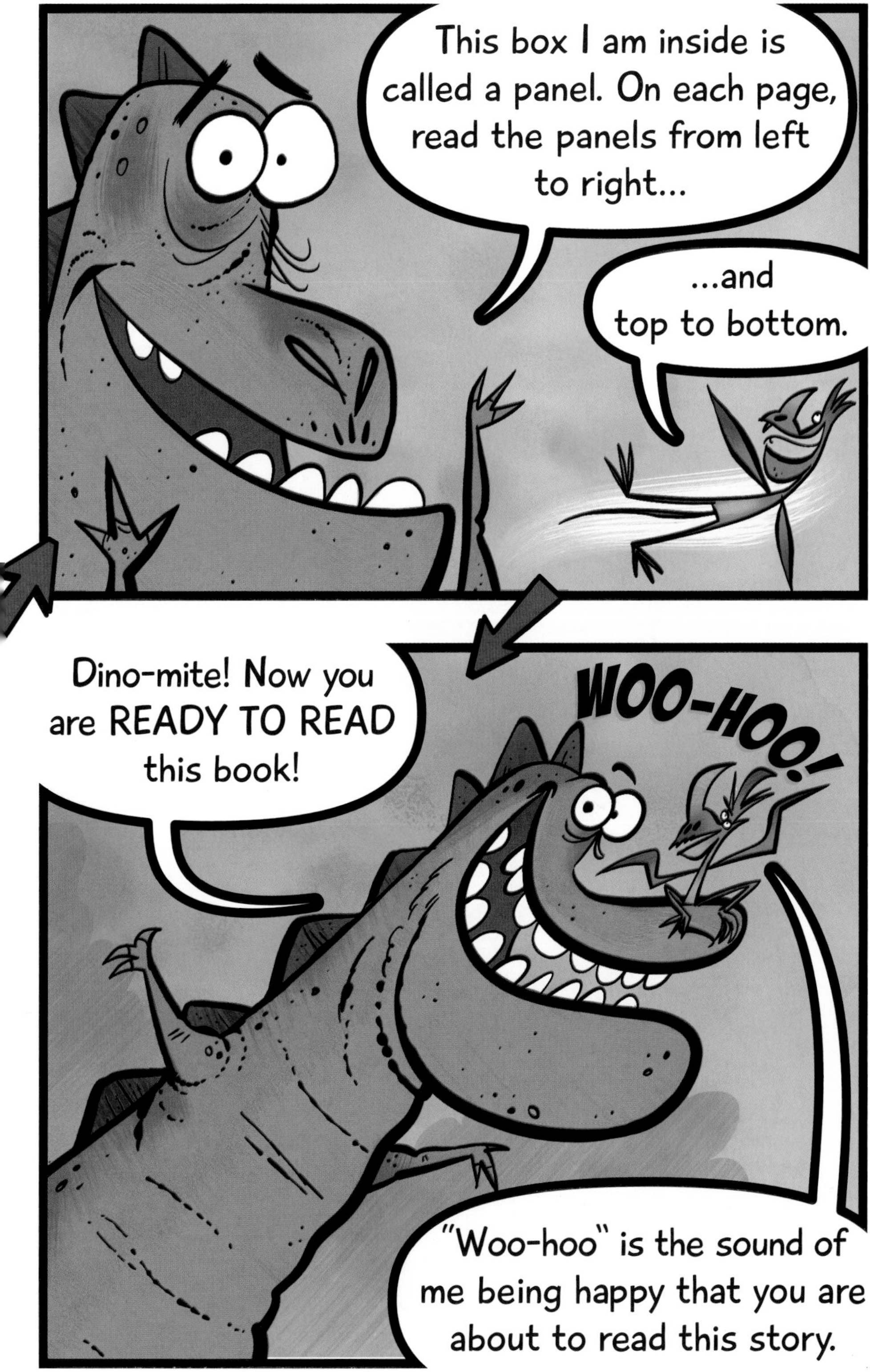
This box I am inside is called a panel. On each page, read the panels from left to right...
...and top to bottom.
Dino-mite! Now you are READY TO READ this book!
WOO-HOO!
"Woo-hoo" is the sound of me being happy that you are about to read this story.

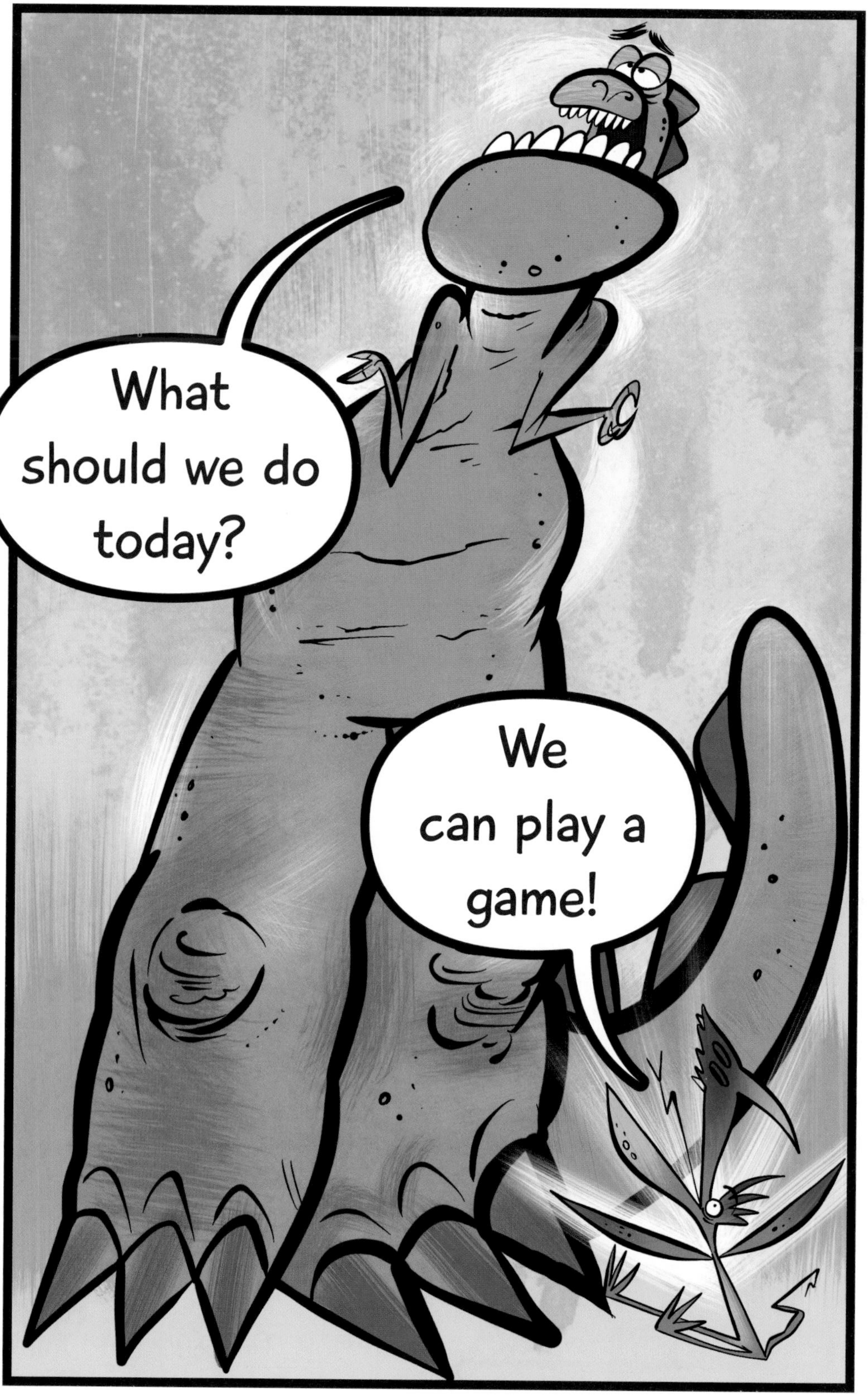
What should we do today?
We can play a game!

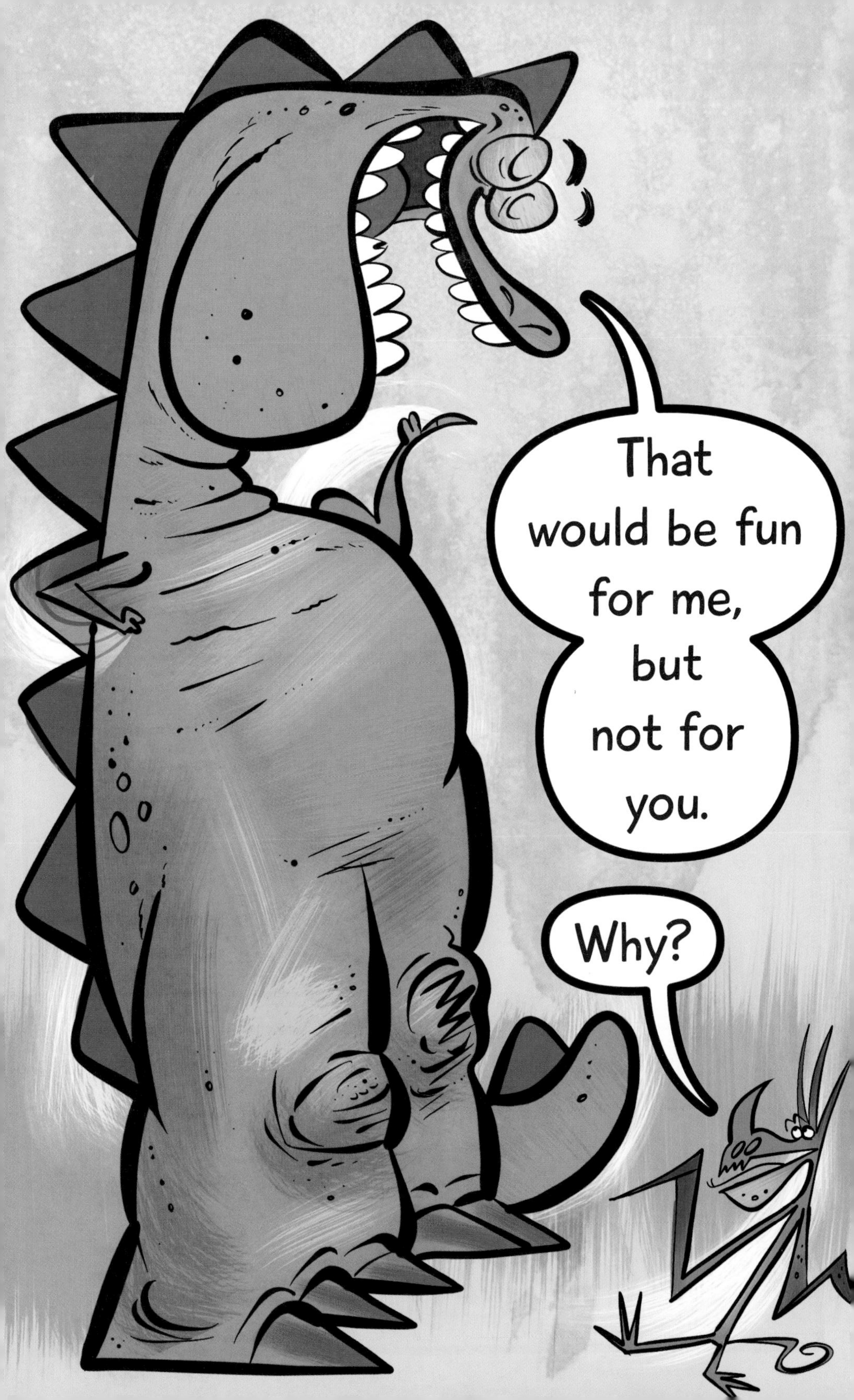
That would be fun for me, but not for you.
Why?

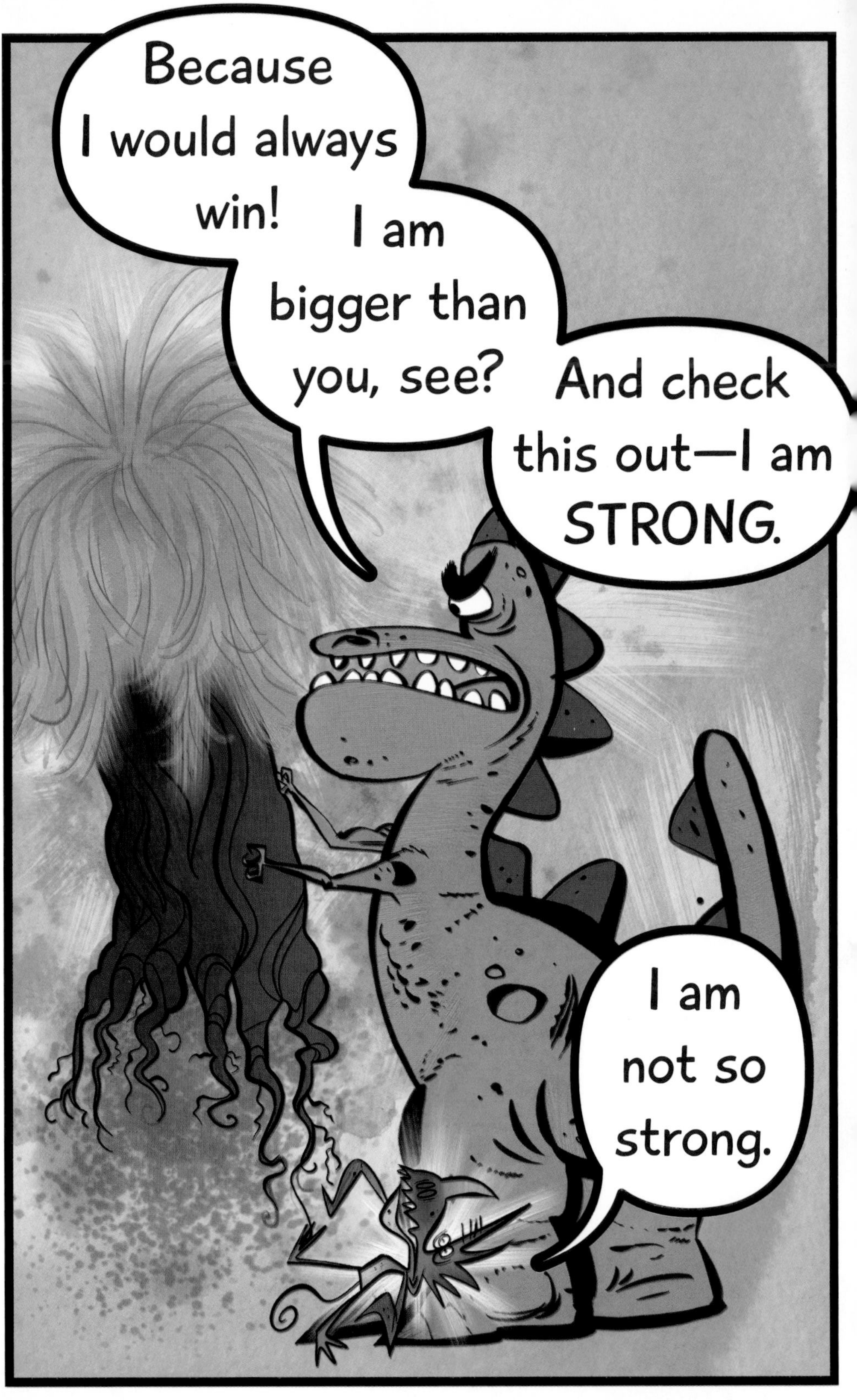
Because I would always win!
I am bigger than you, see?
And check this out—I am STRONG.
I am not so strong.

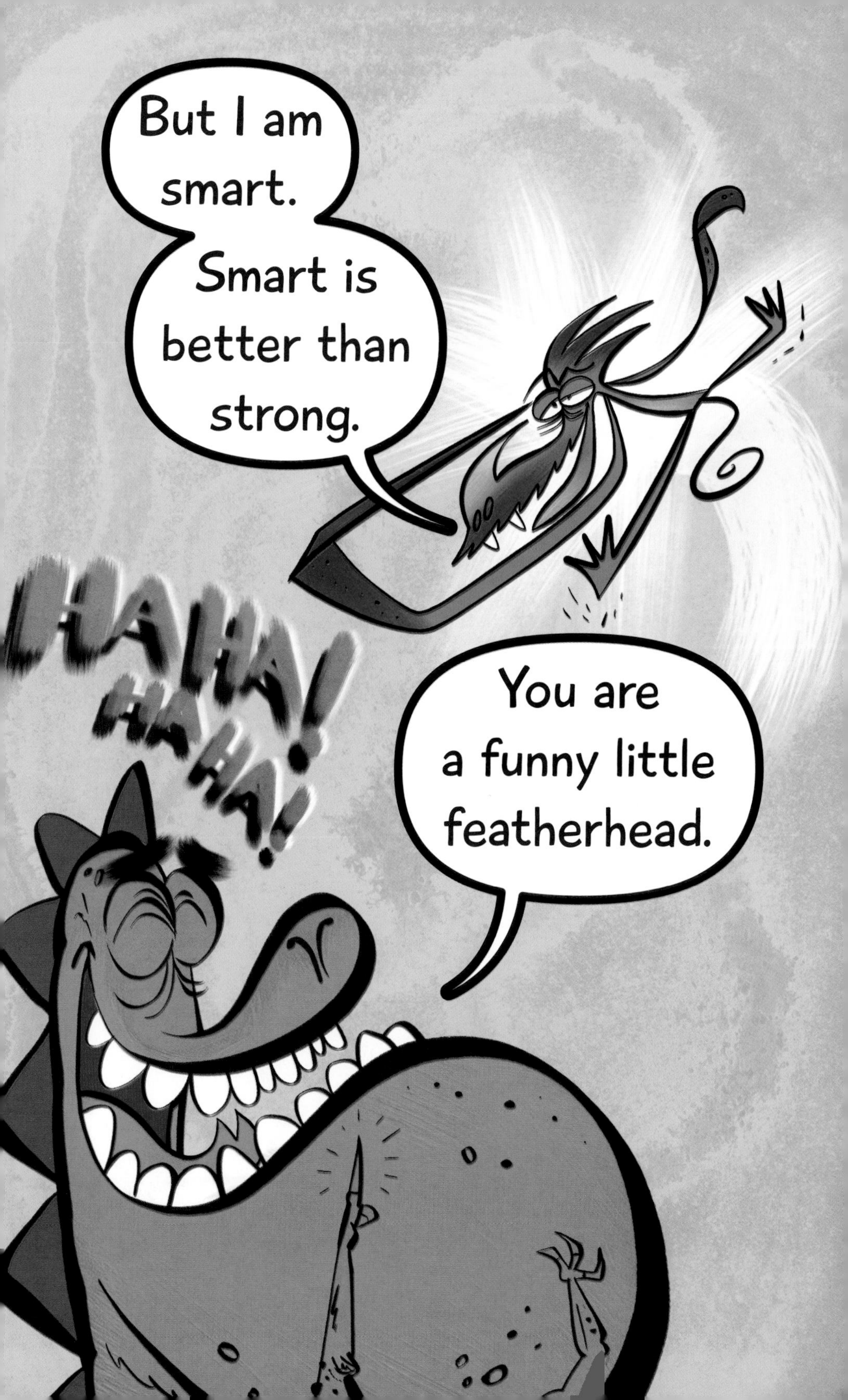
But I am smart.
Smart is better than strong.
HA HA! HA HA! HA!
You are a funny little featherhead.

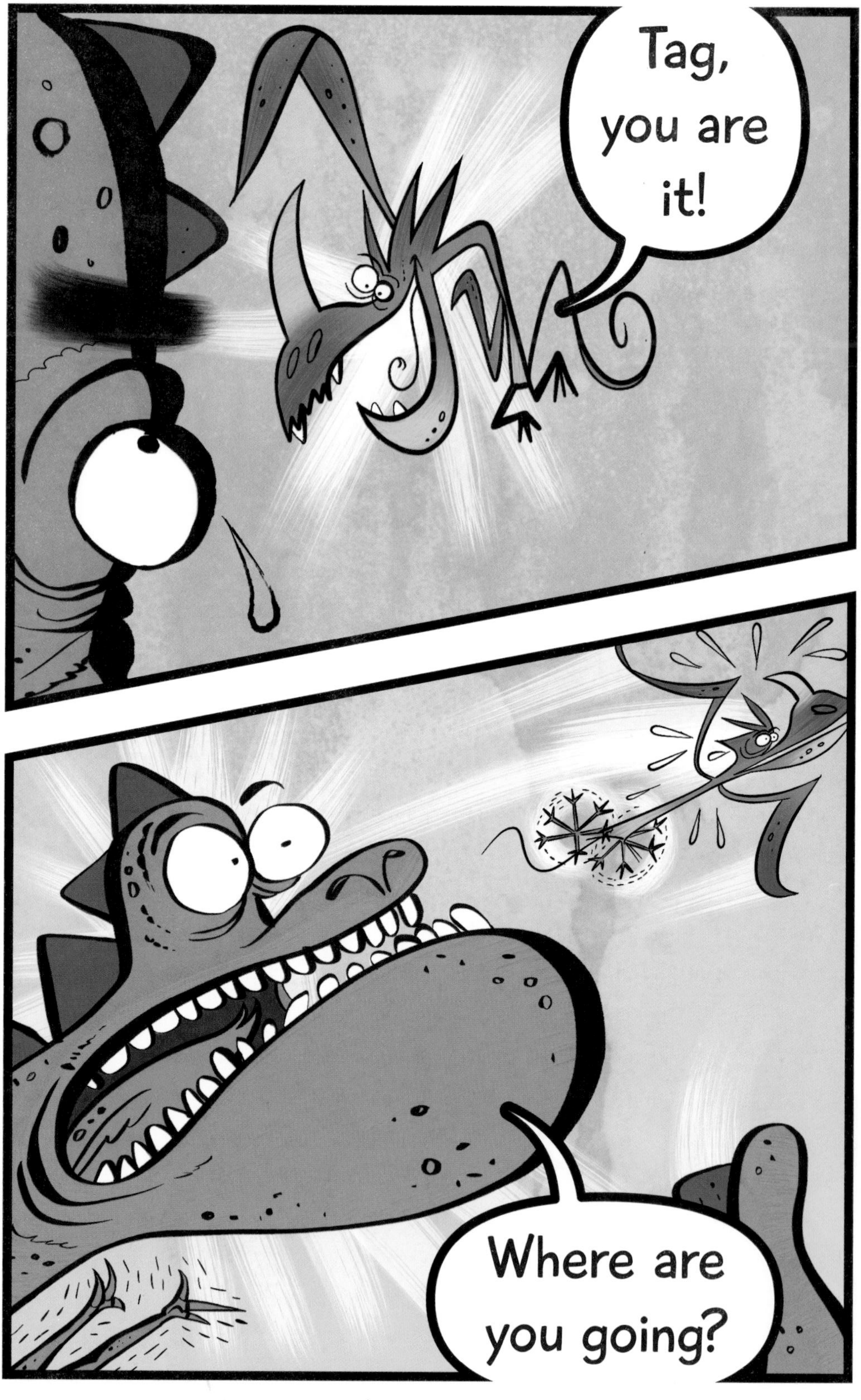
Tag, you are it!
Where are you going?

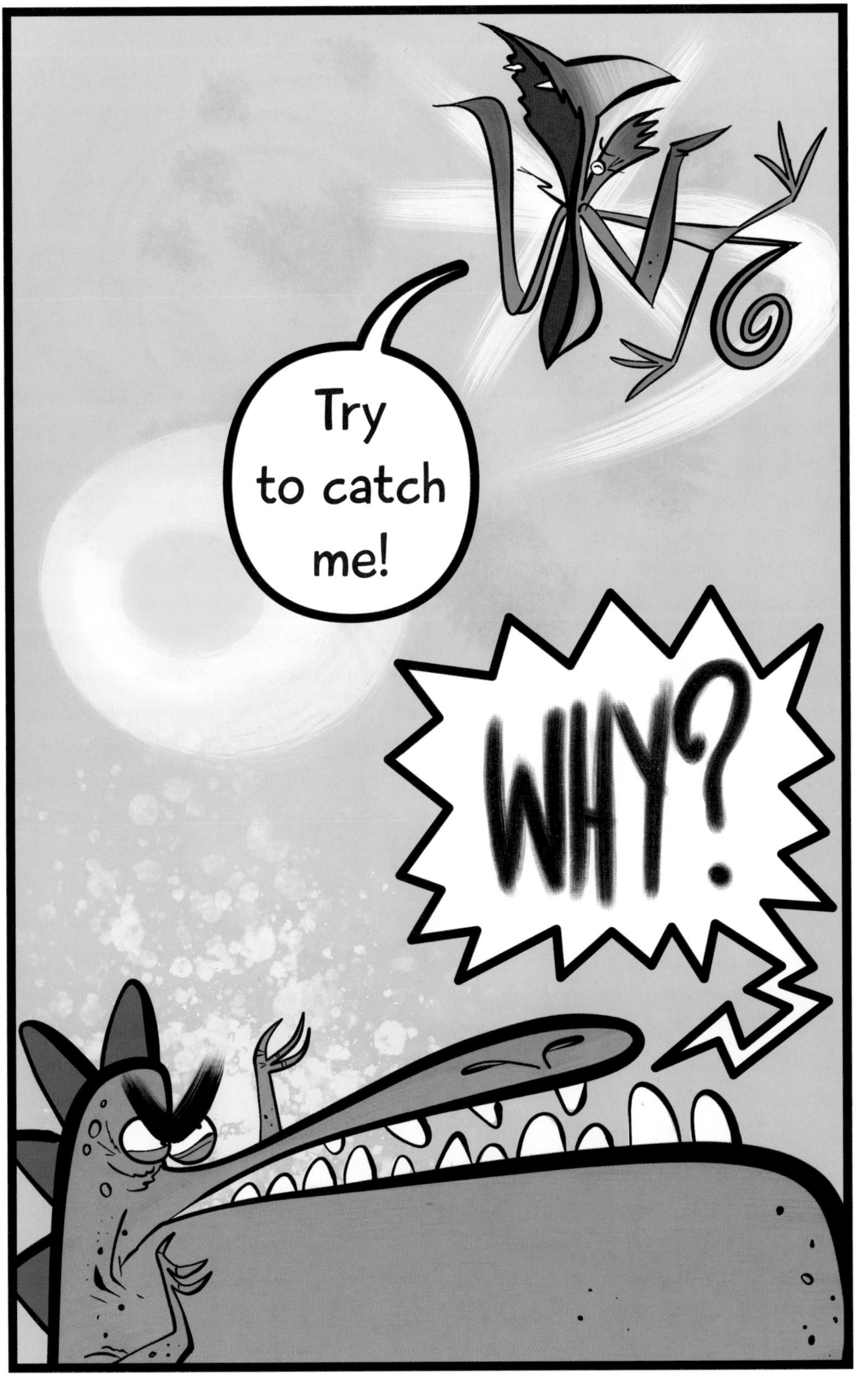
Try to catch me!
WHY?

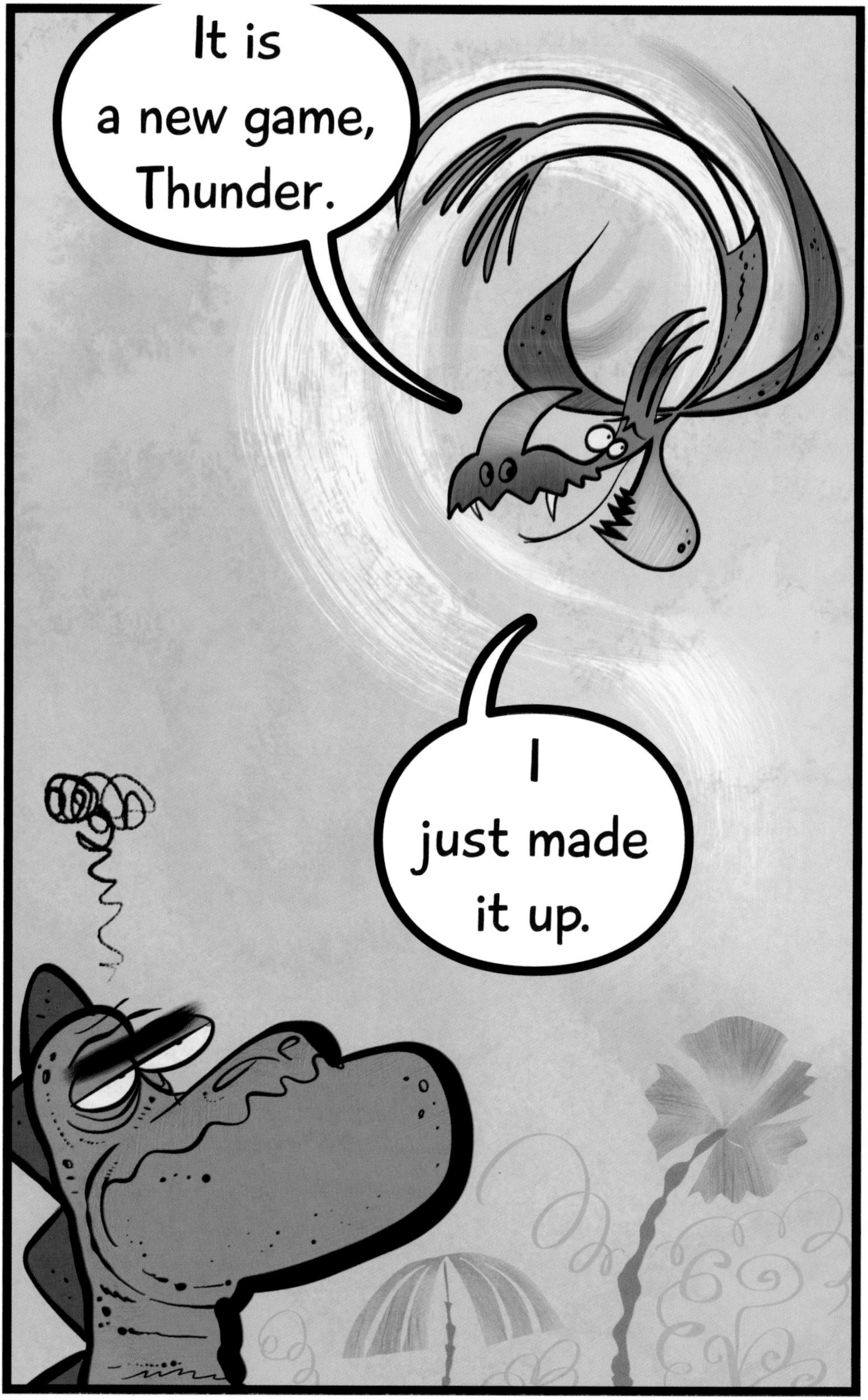
It is a new game, Thunder.
I just made it up.

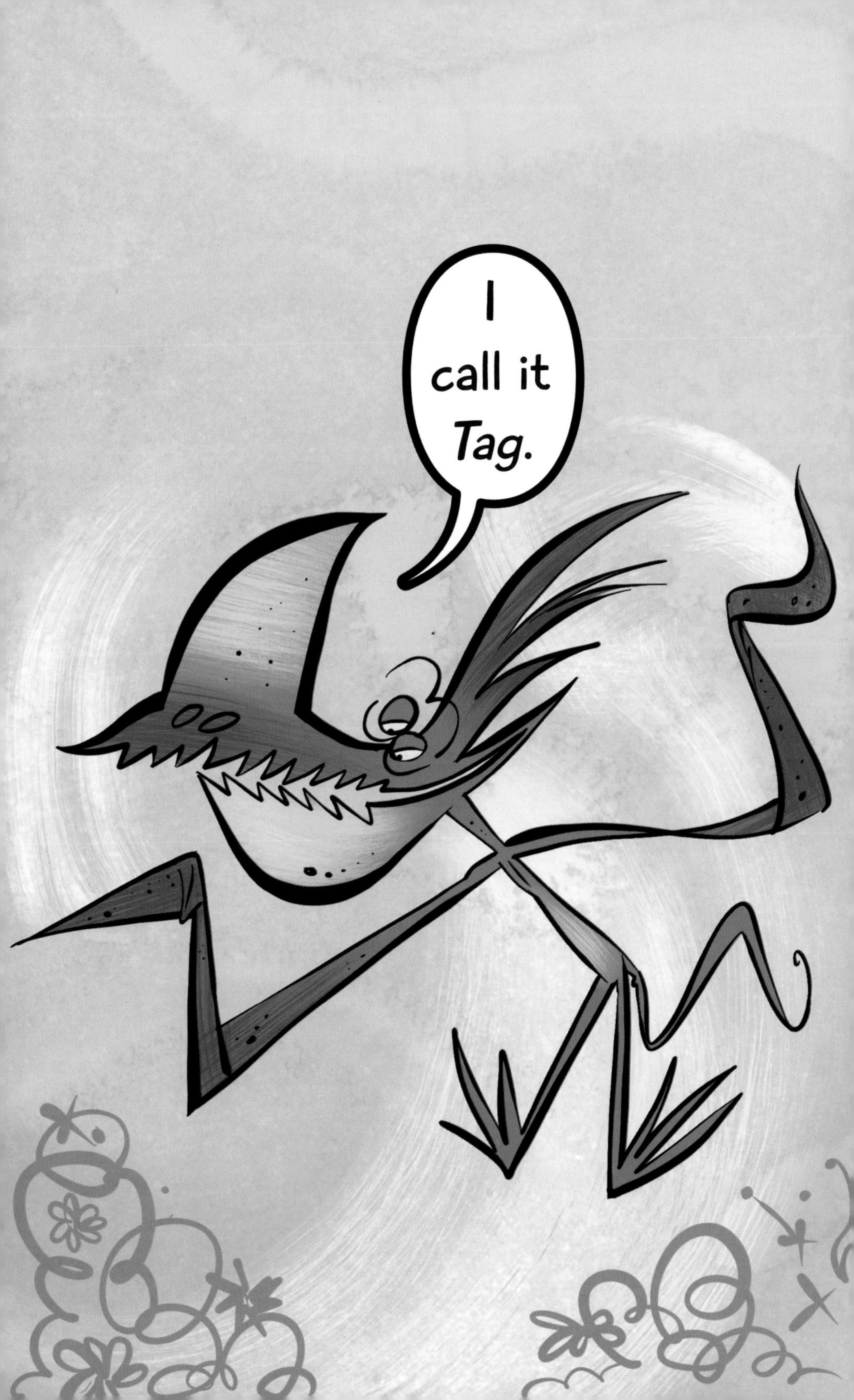
I call it *Tag.*

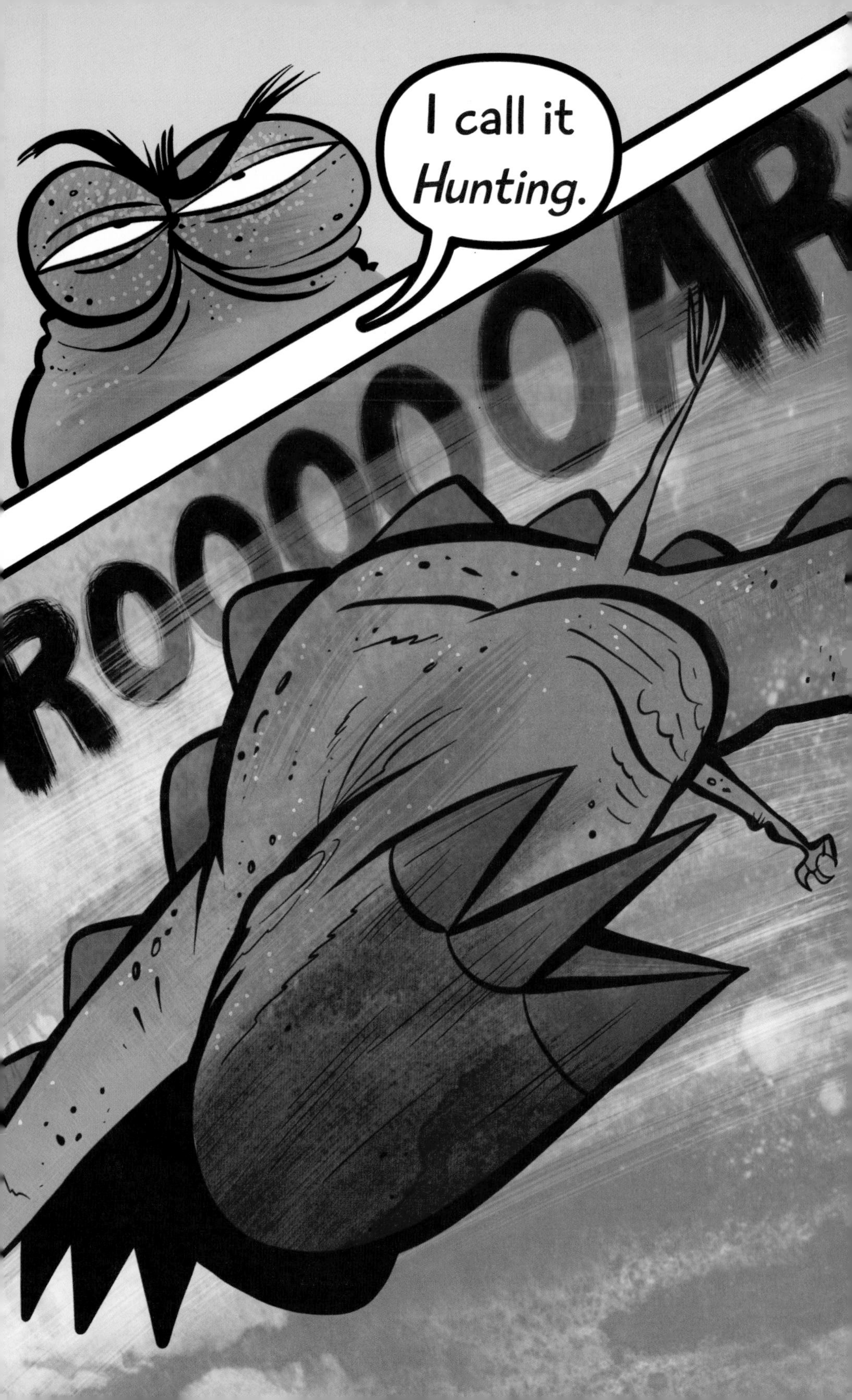
I call it *Hunting.*
ROOOOOOAR

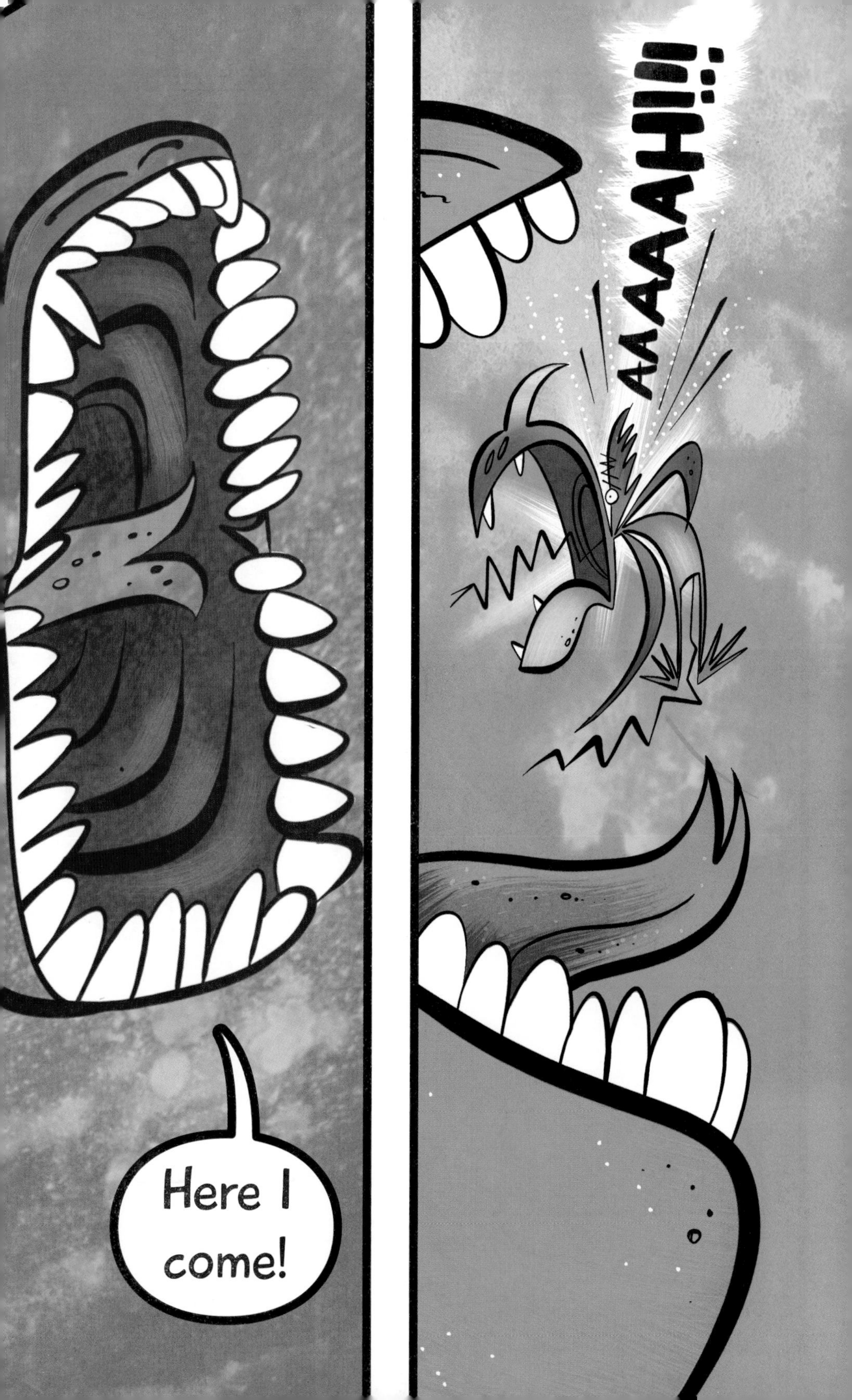
Here I come!
AAAAAH!!!

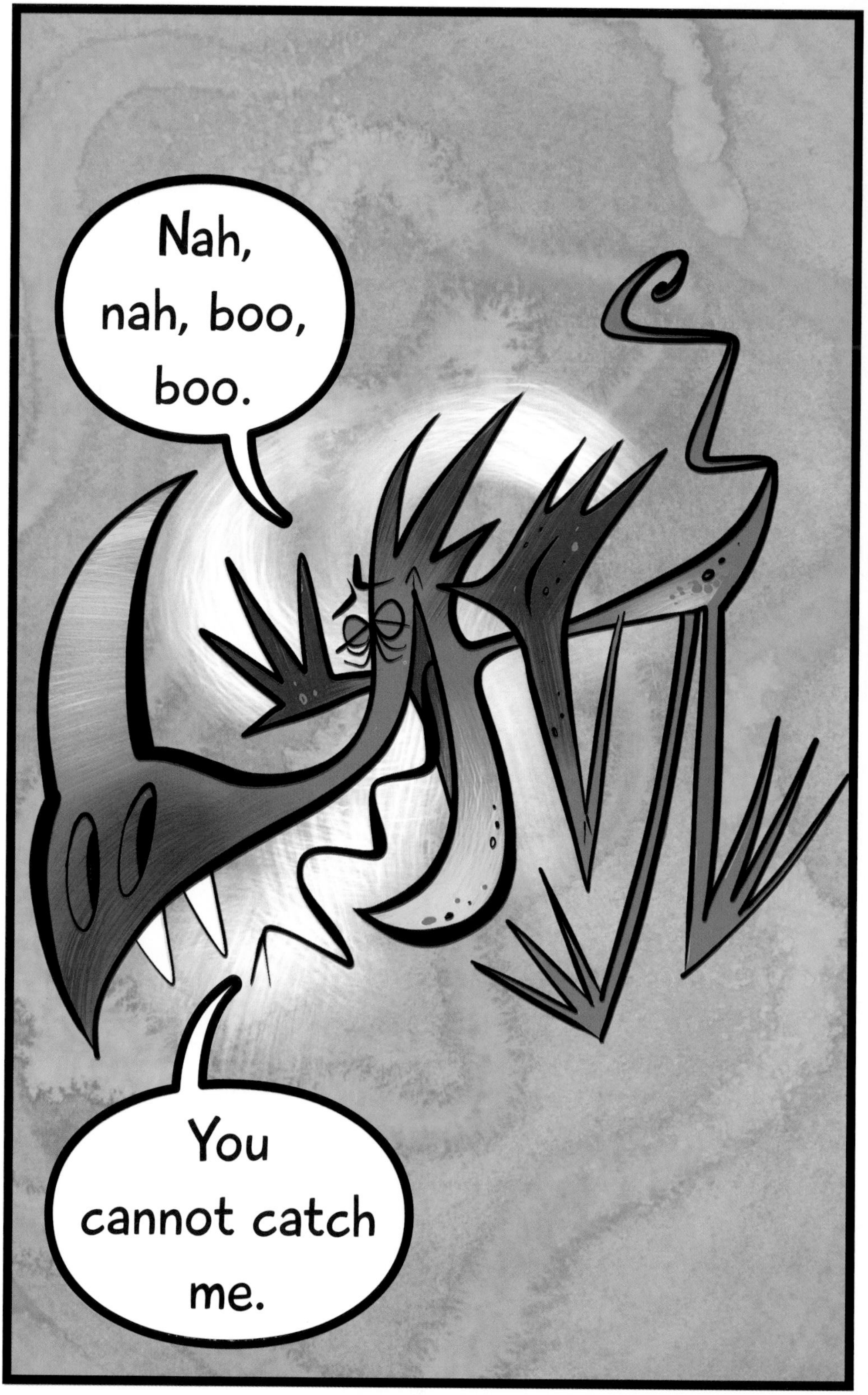
Nah, nah, boo, boo.
You cannot catch me.

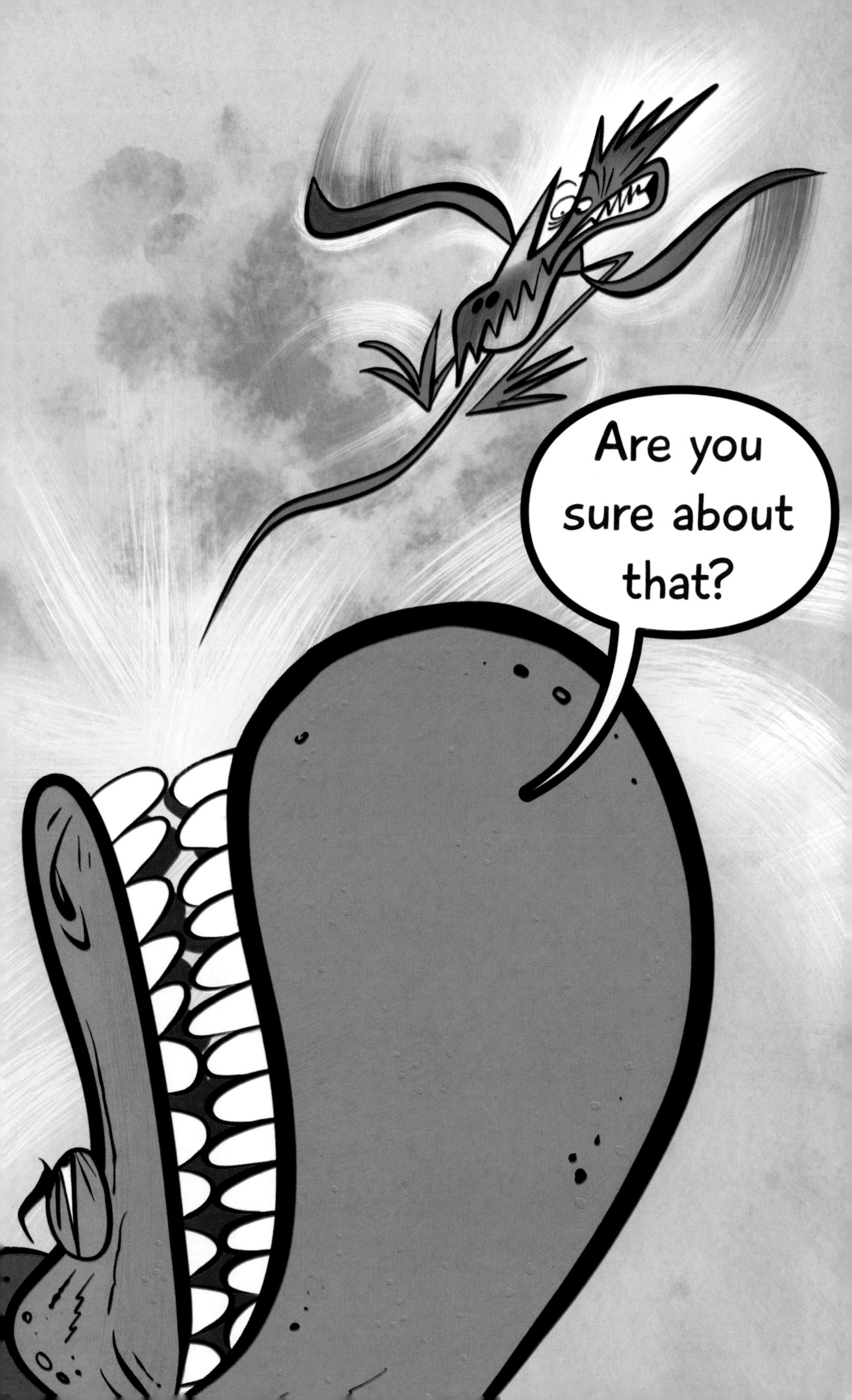
Are you sure about that?

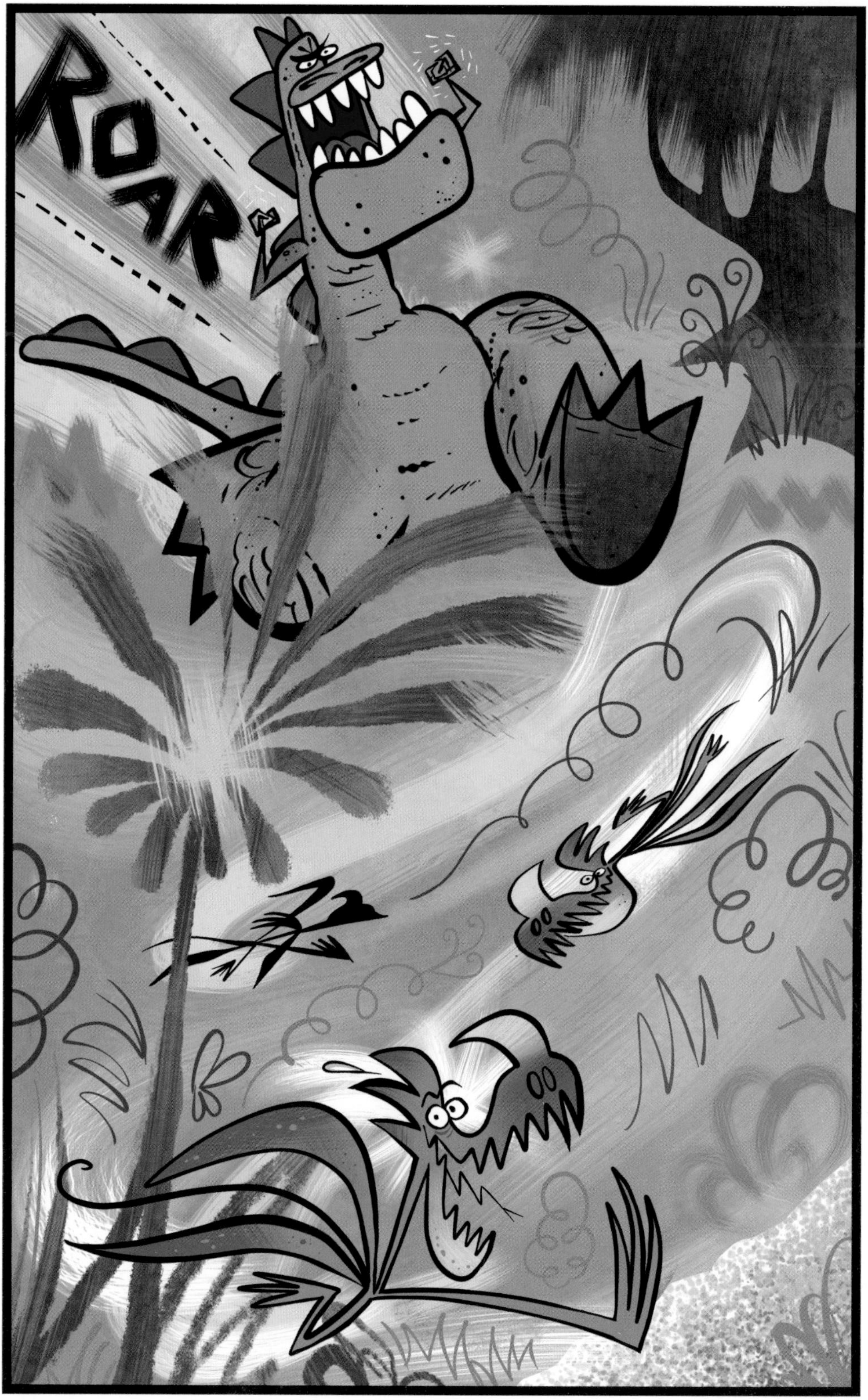
ROAR

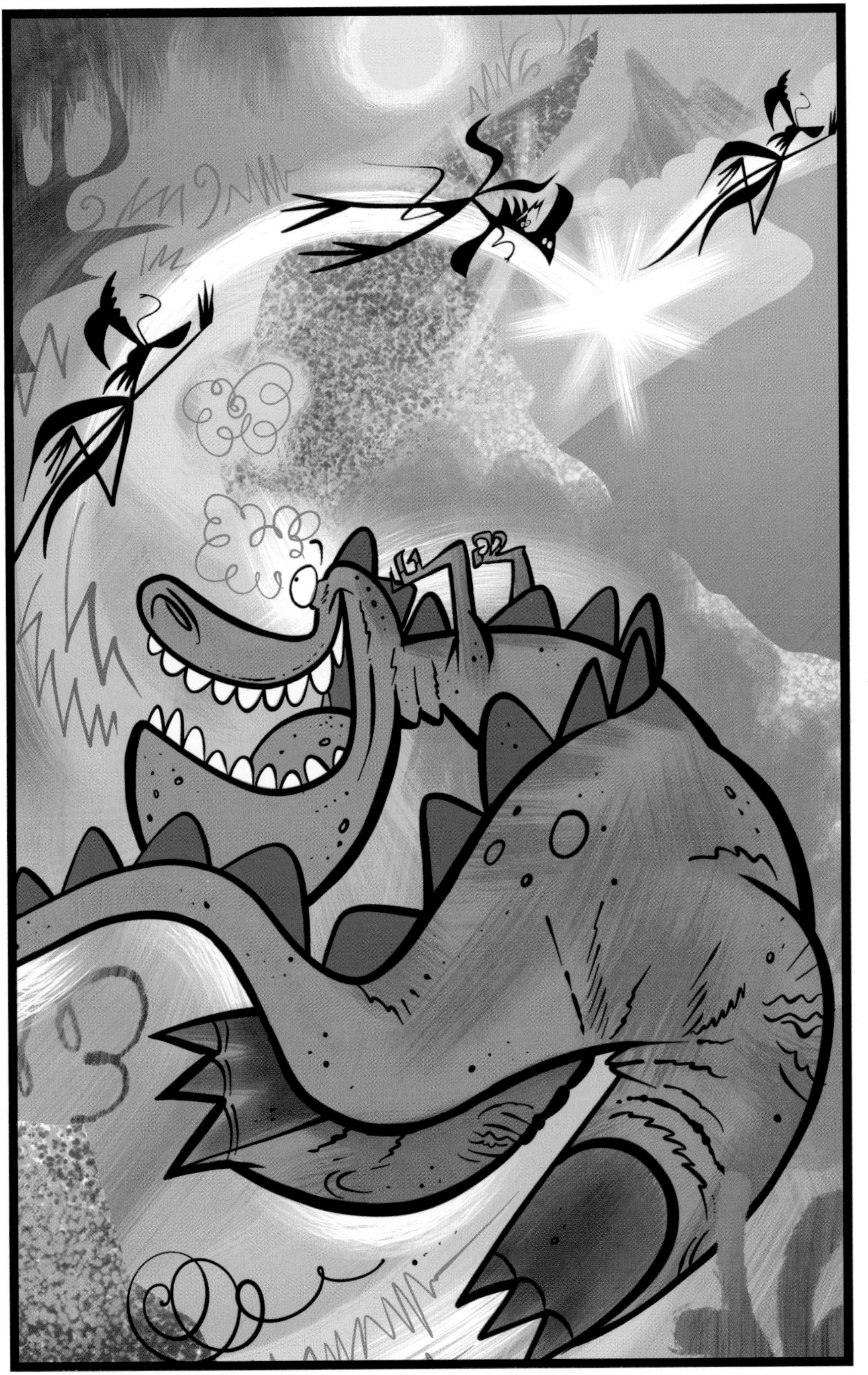

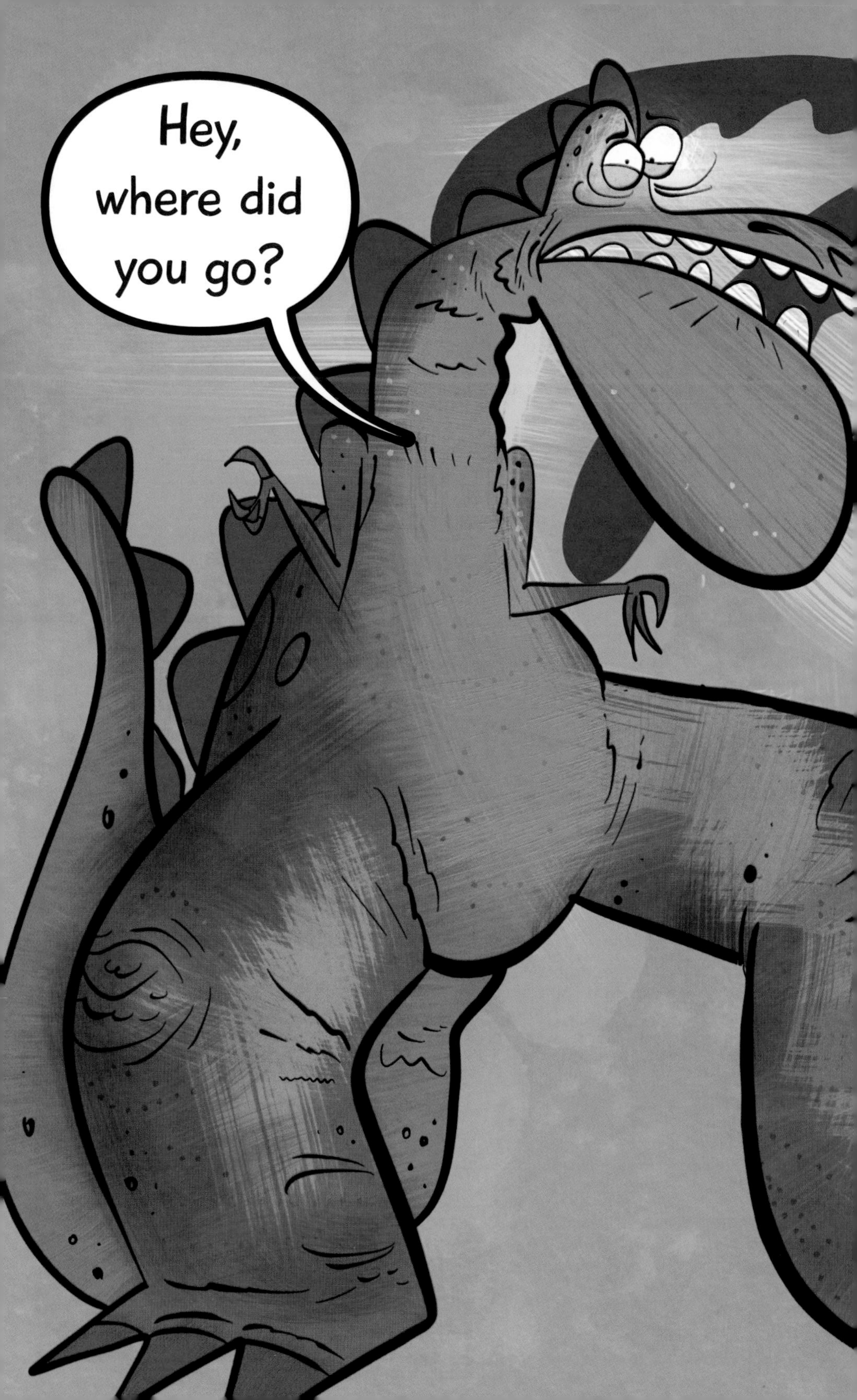
Hey, where did you go?

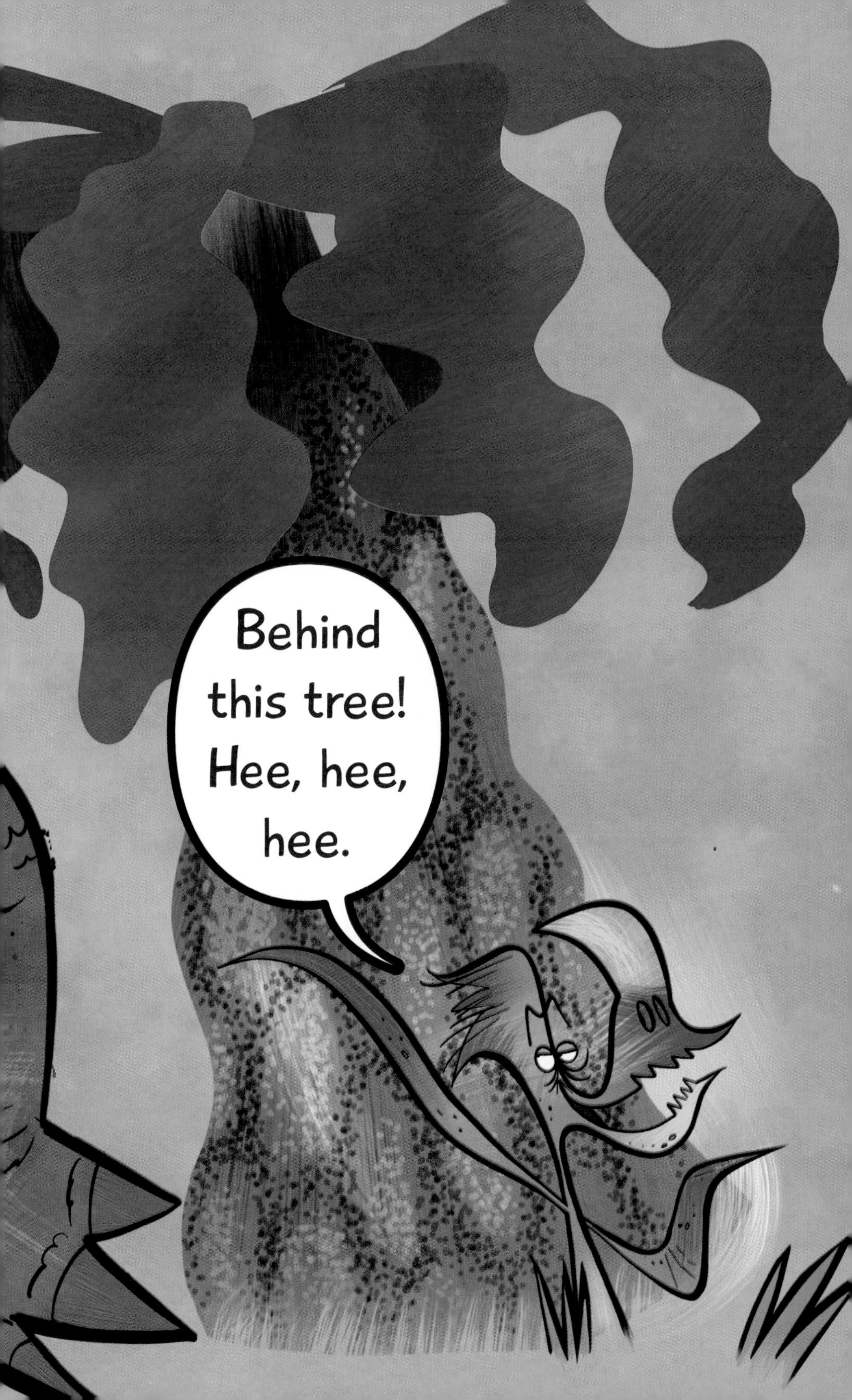
Behind this tree! Hee, hee, hee.

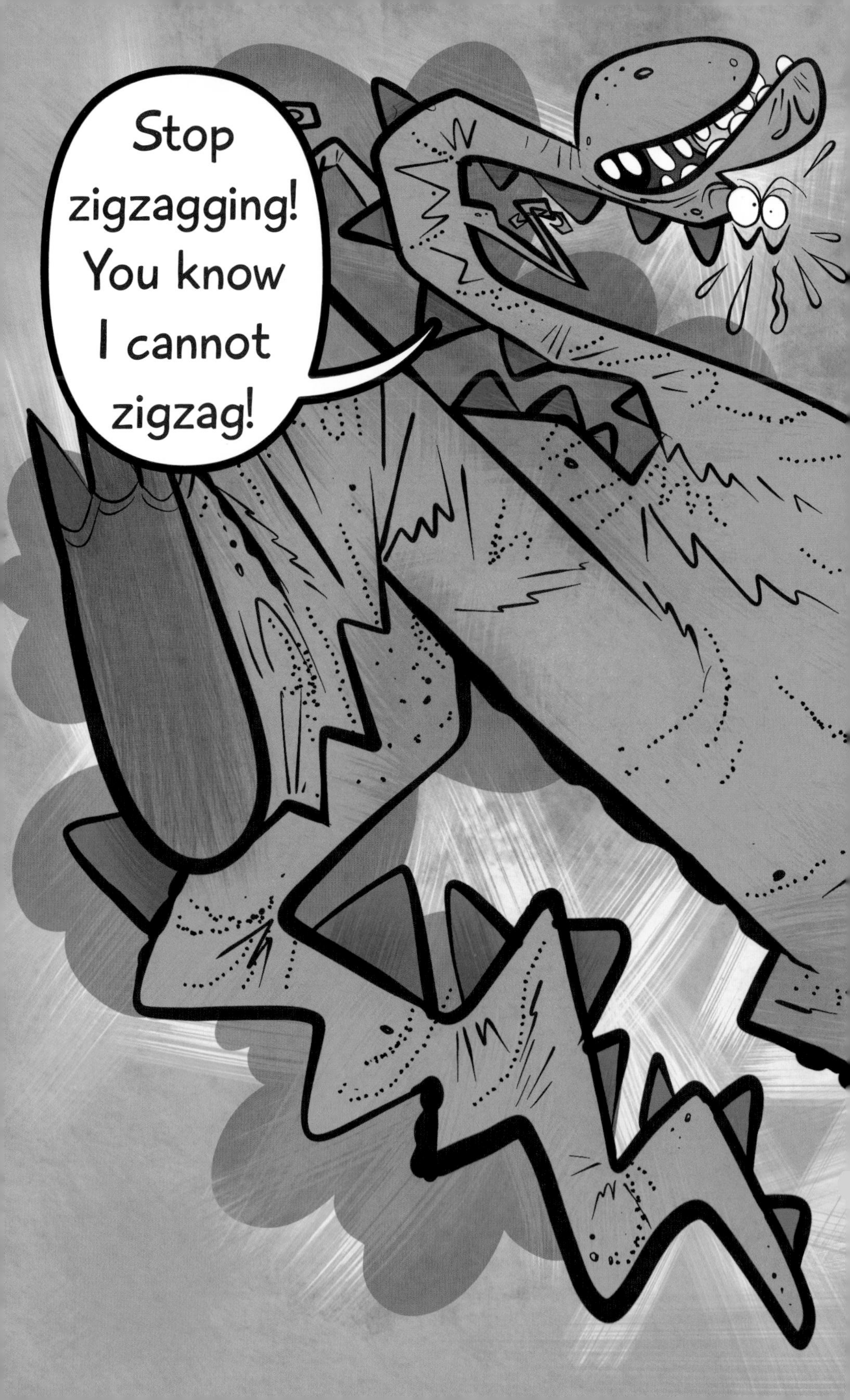
Stop zigzagging! You know I cannot zigzag!

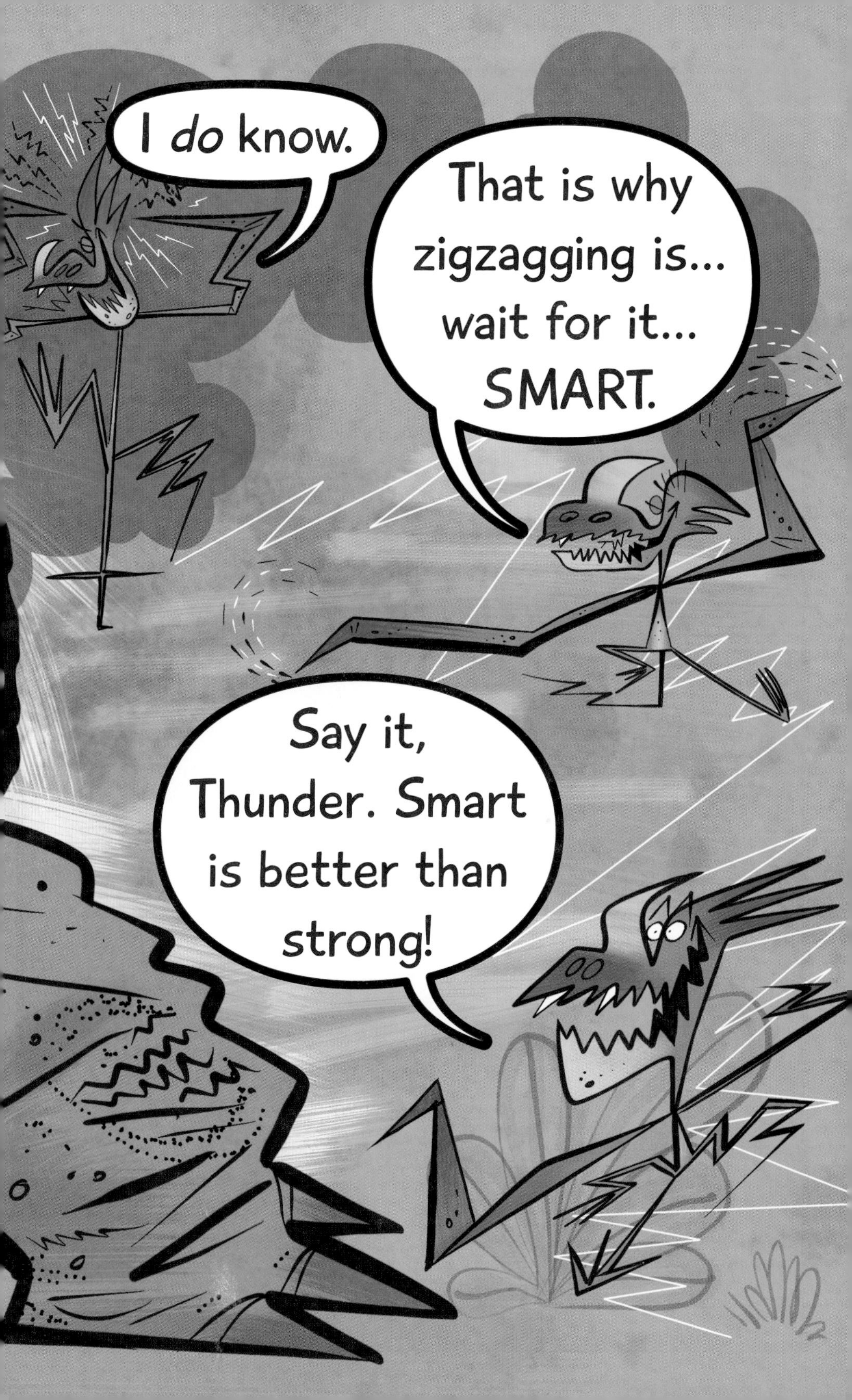
I *do* know.
That is why zigzagging is... wait for it... SMART.
Say it, Thunder. Smart is better than strong!

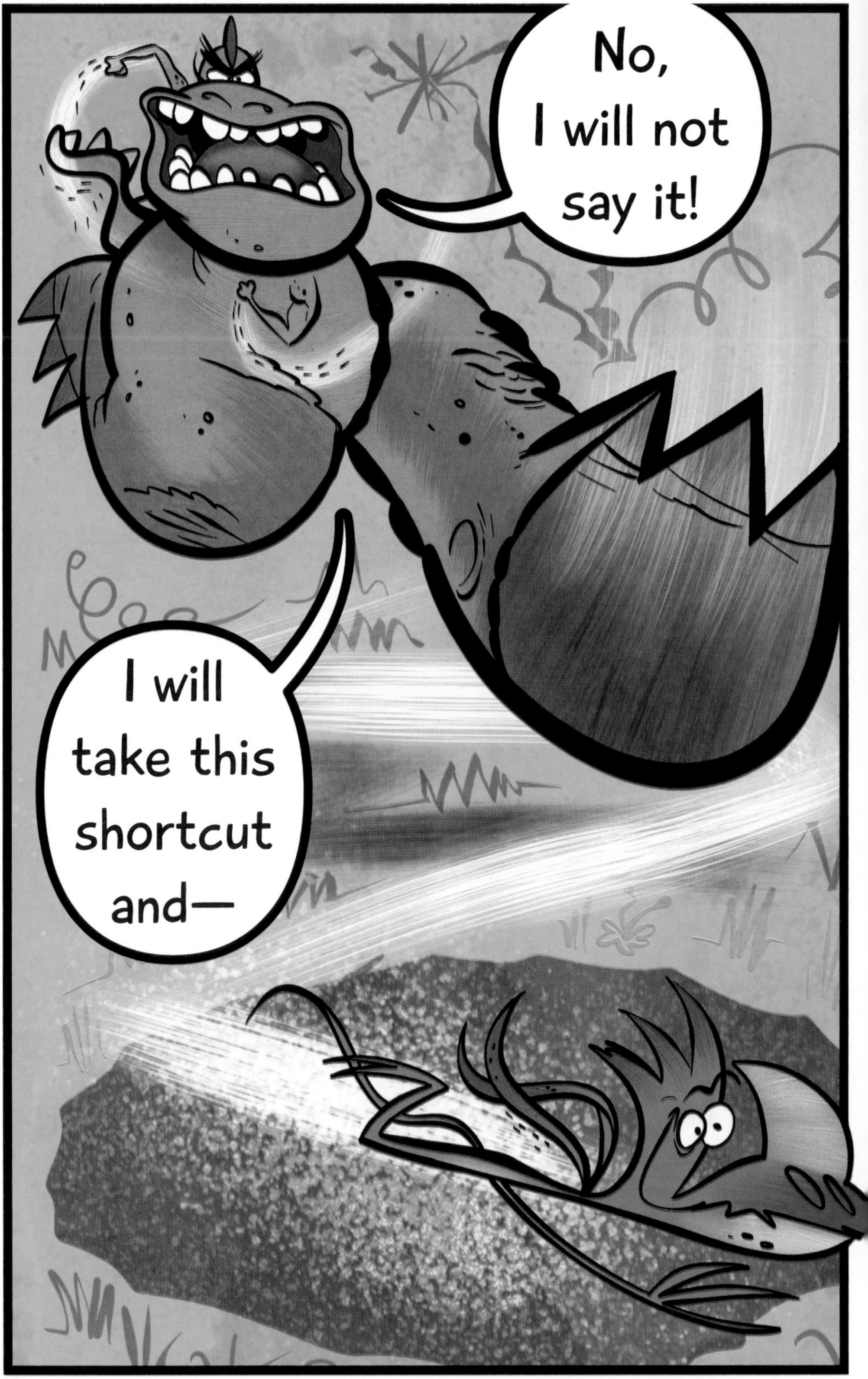
No, I will not say it!
I will take this shortcut and—

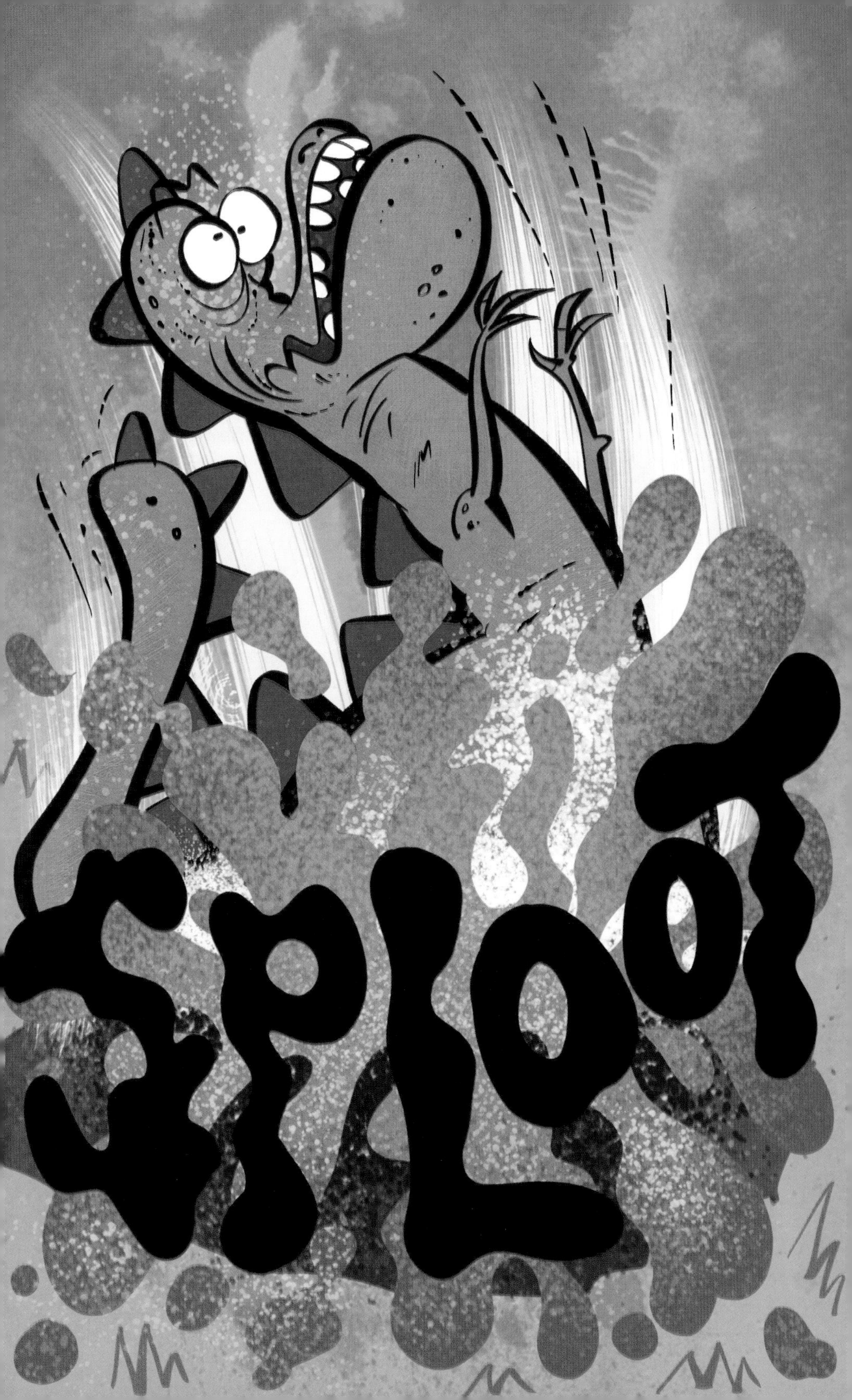
SPLOOT

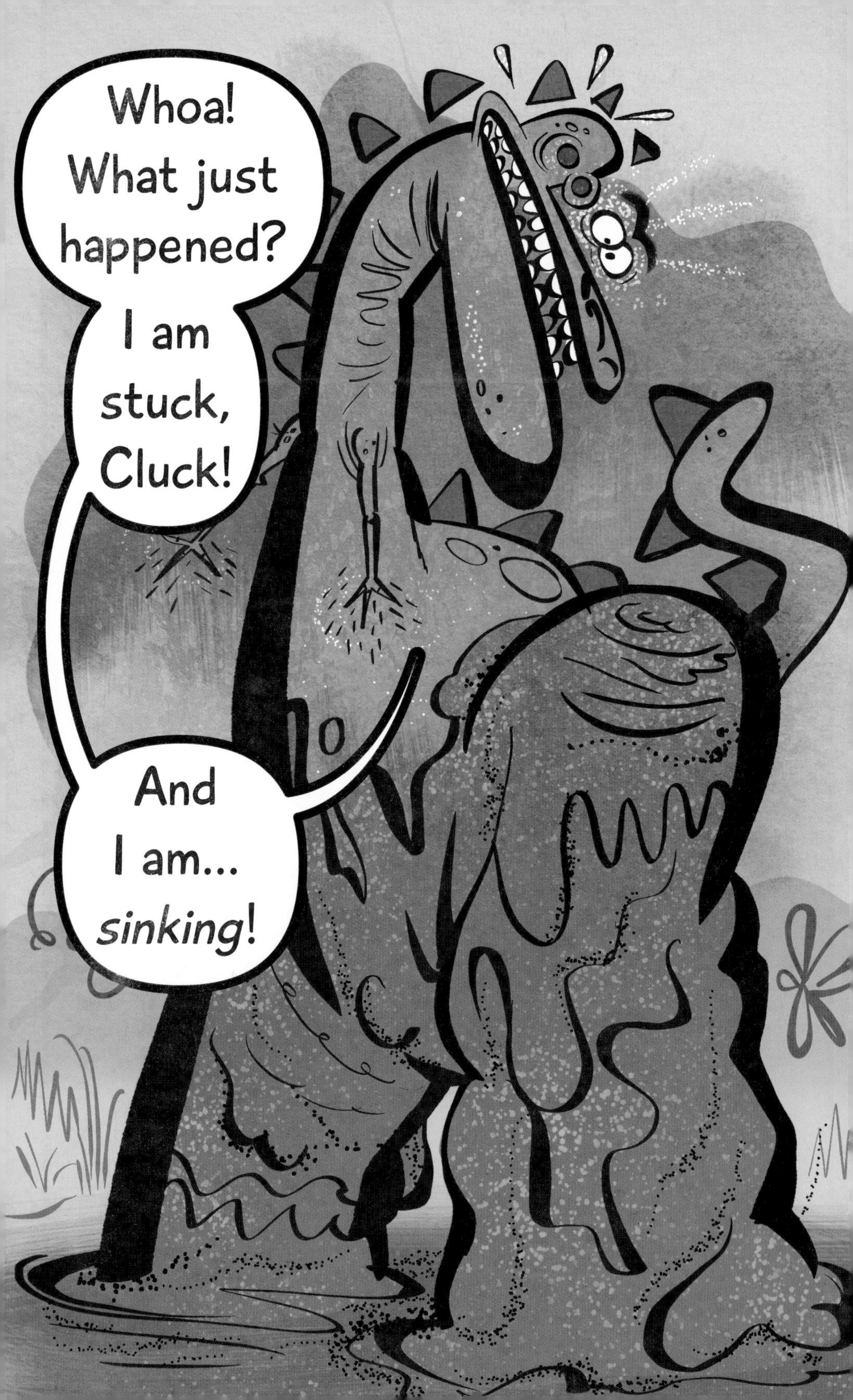
Whoa! What just happened?
I am stuck, Cluck!
And I am... *sinking*!

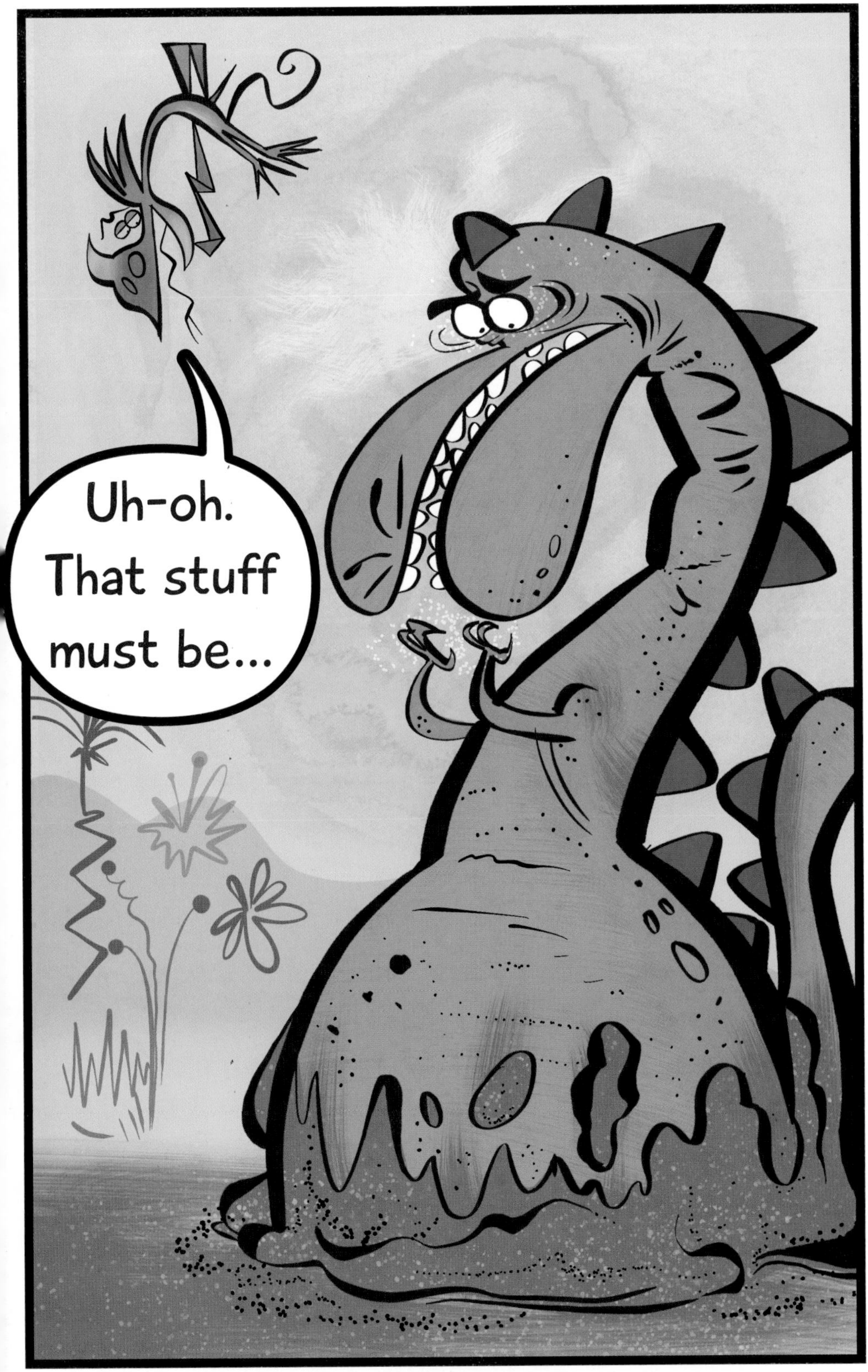
Uh-oh. That stuff must be...

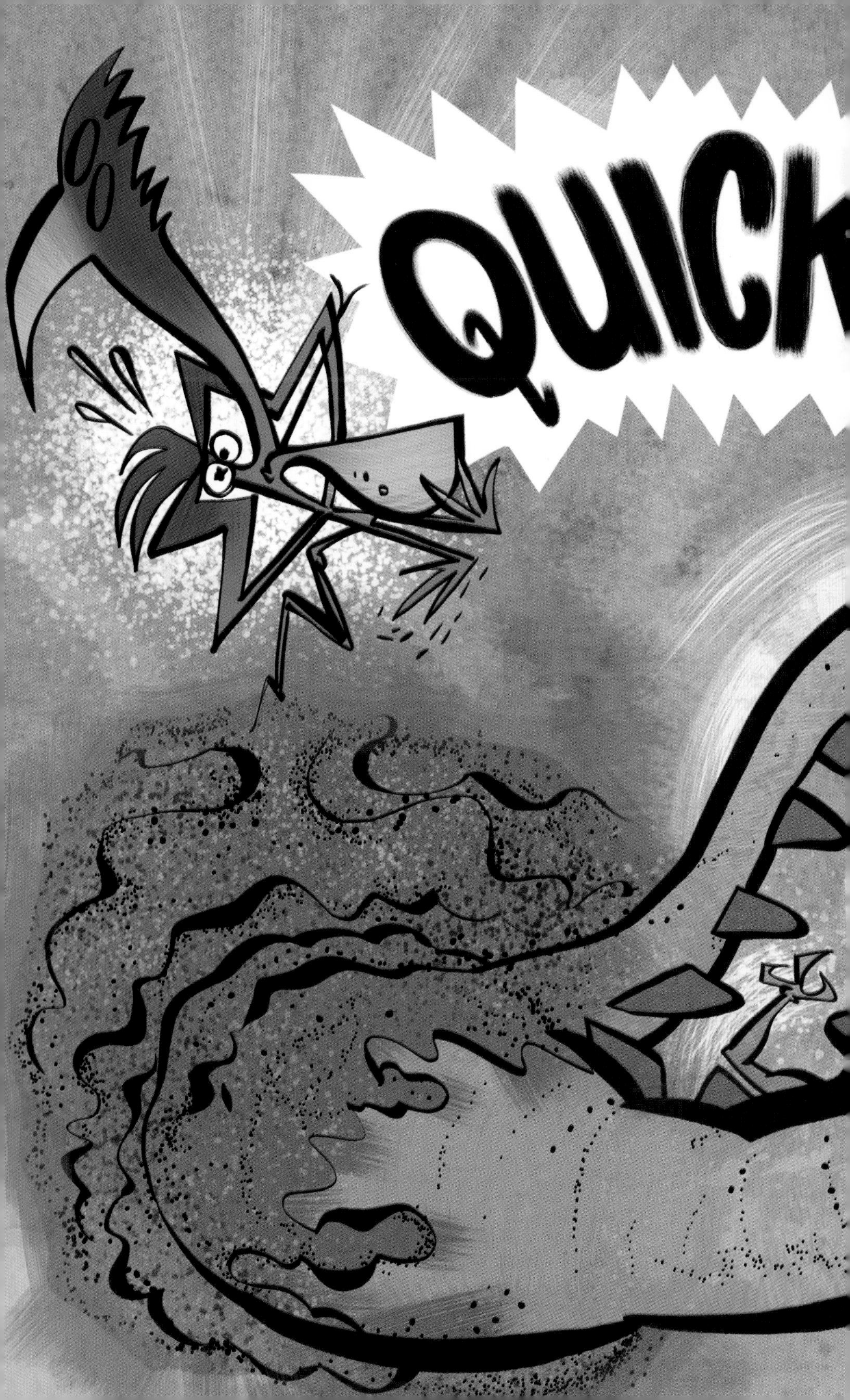
QUICK

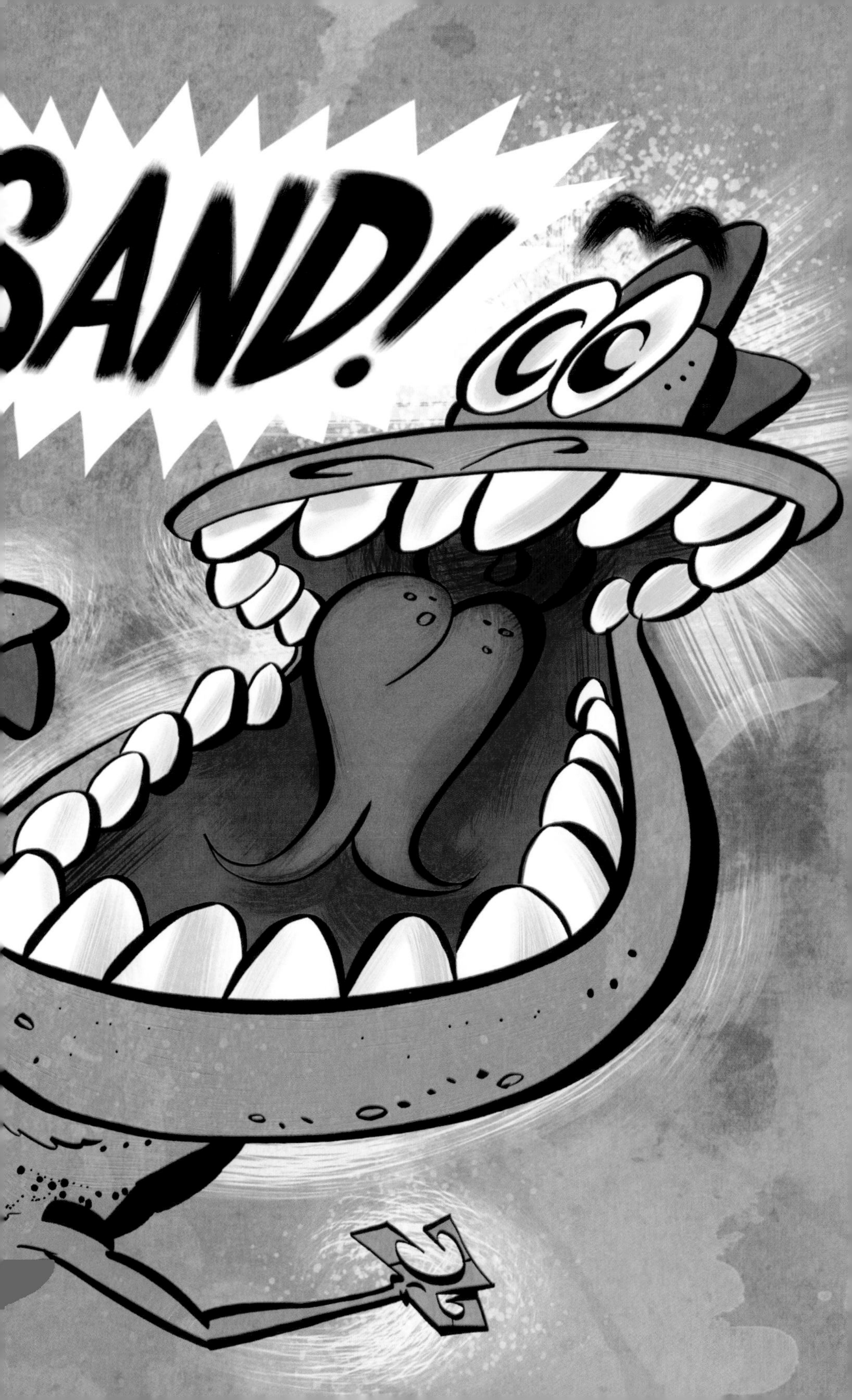

BAND!

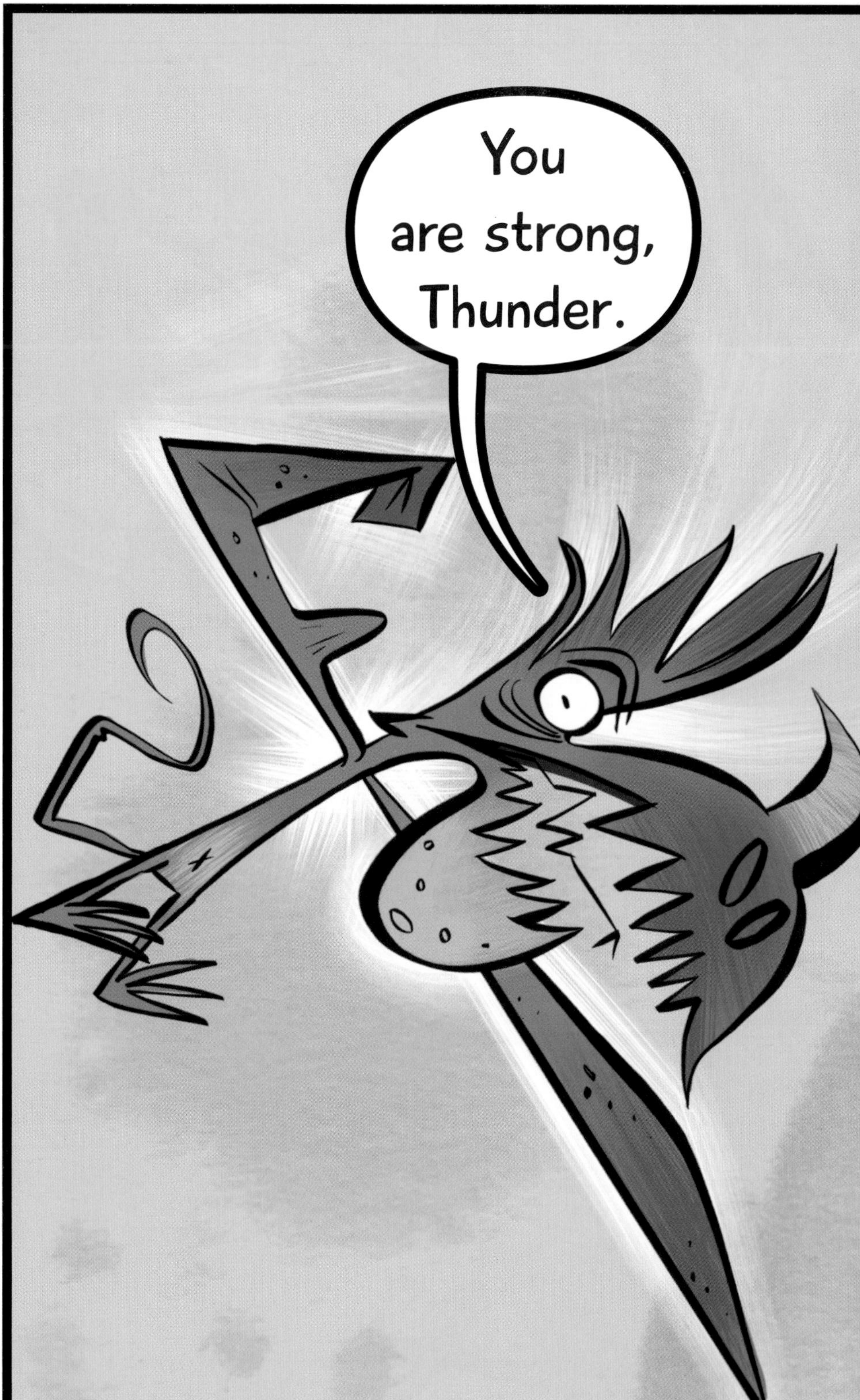
You are strong, Thunder.

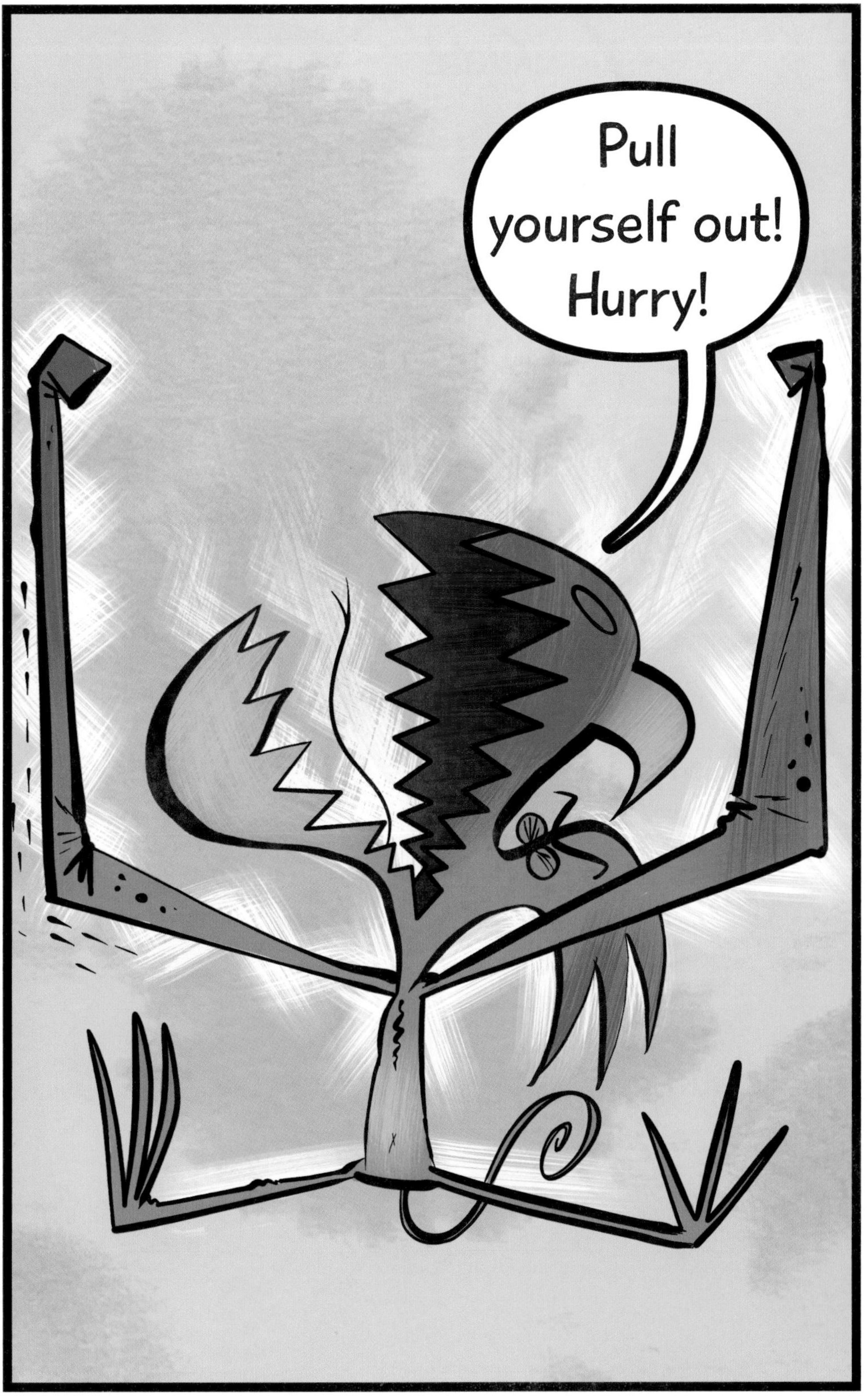
Pull yourself out! Hurry!

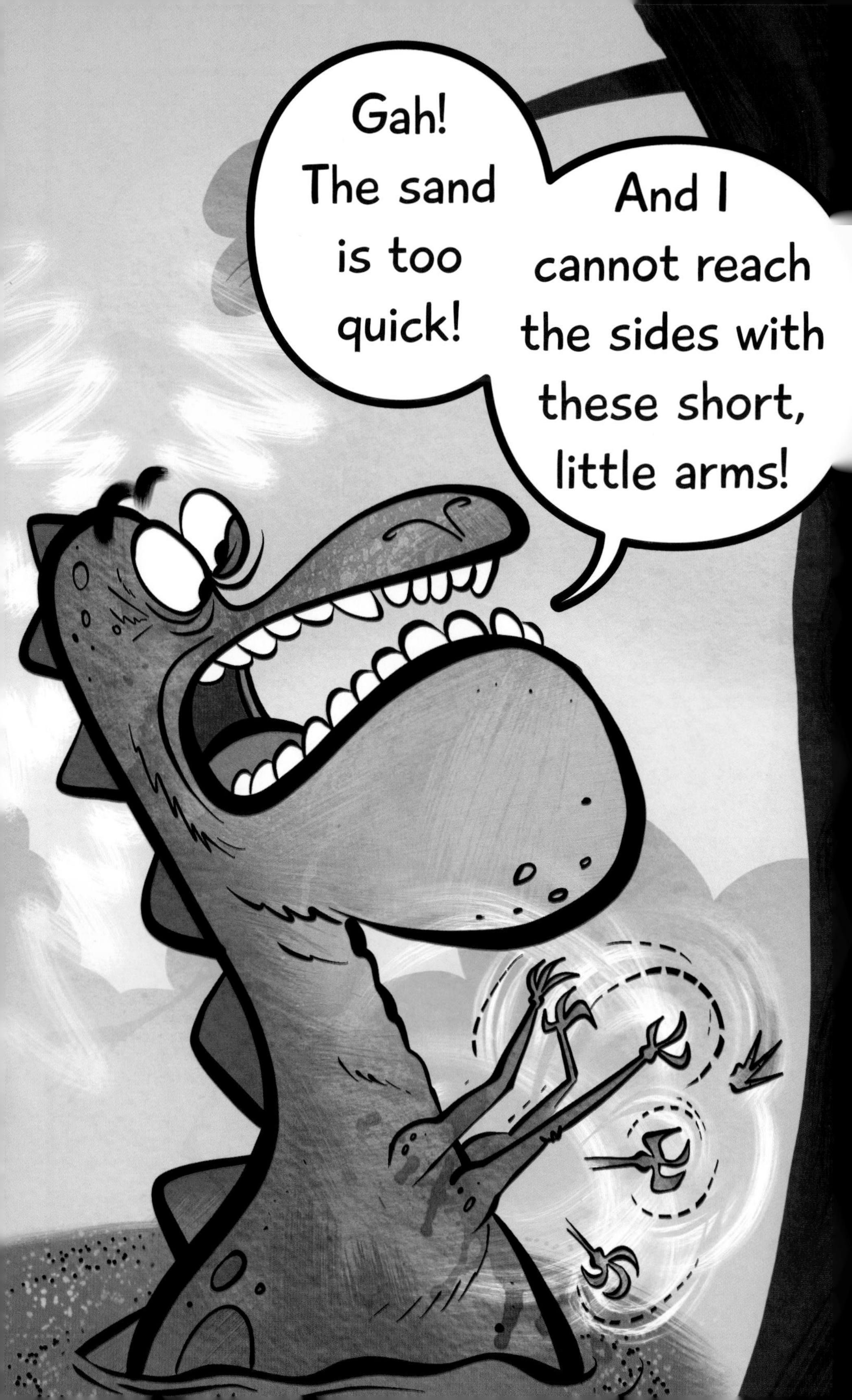
Gah! The sand is too quick!
And I cannot reach the sides with these short, little arms!

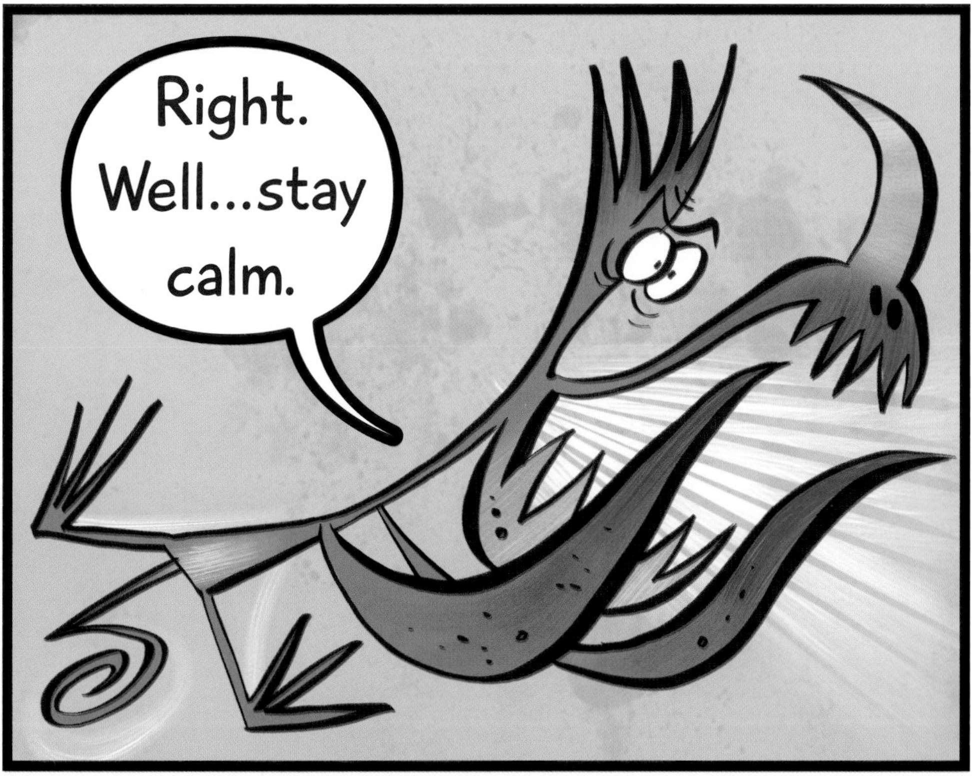
Right. Well...stay calm.

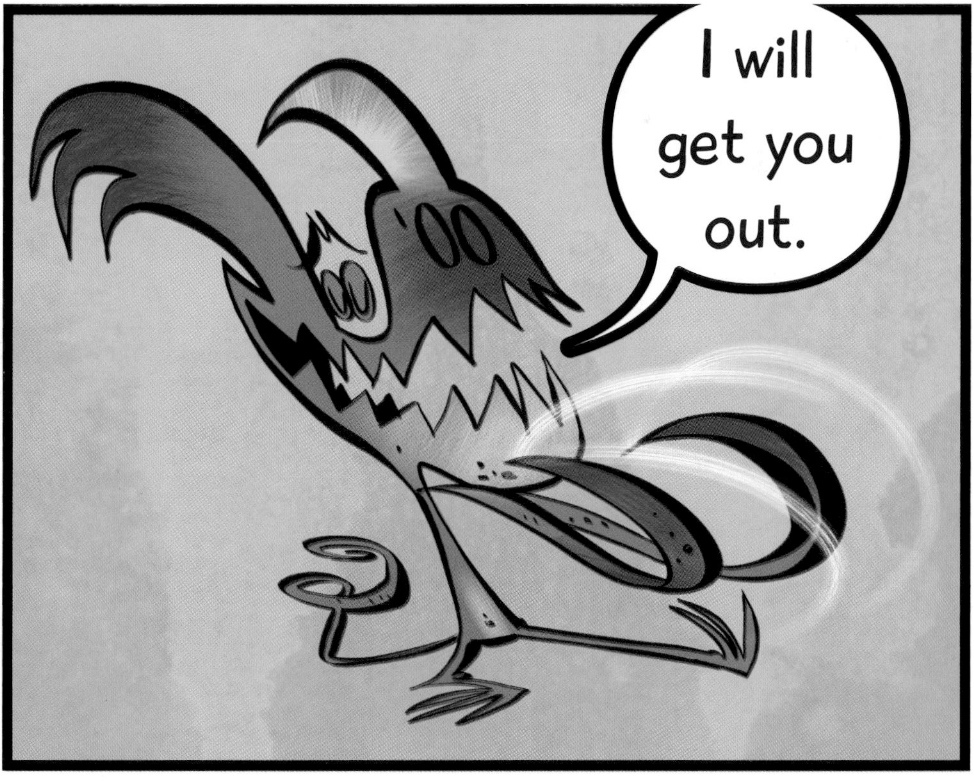
I will get you out.

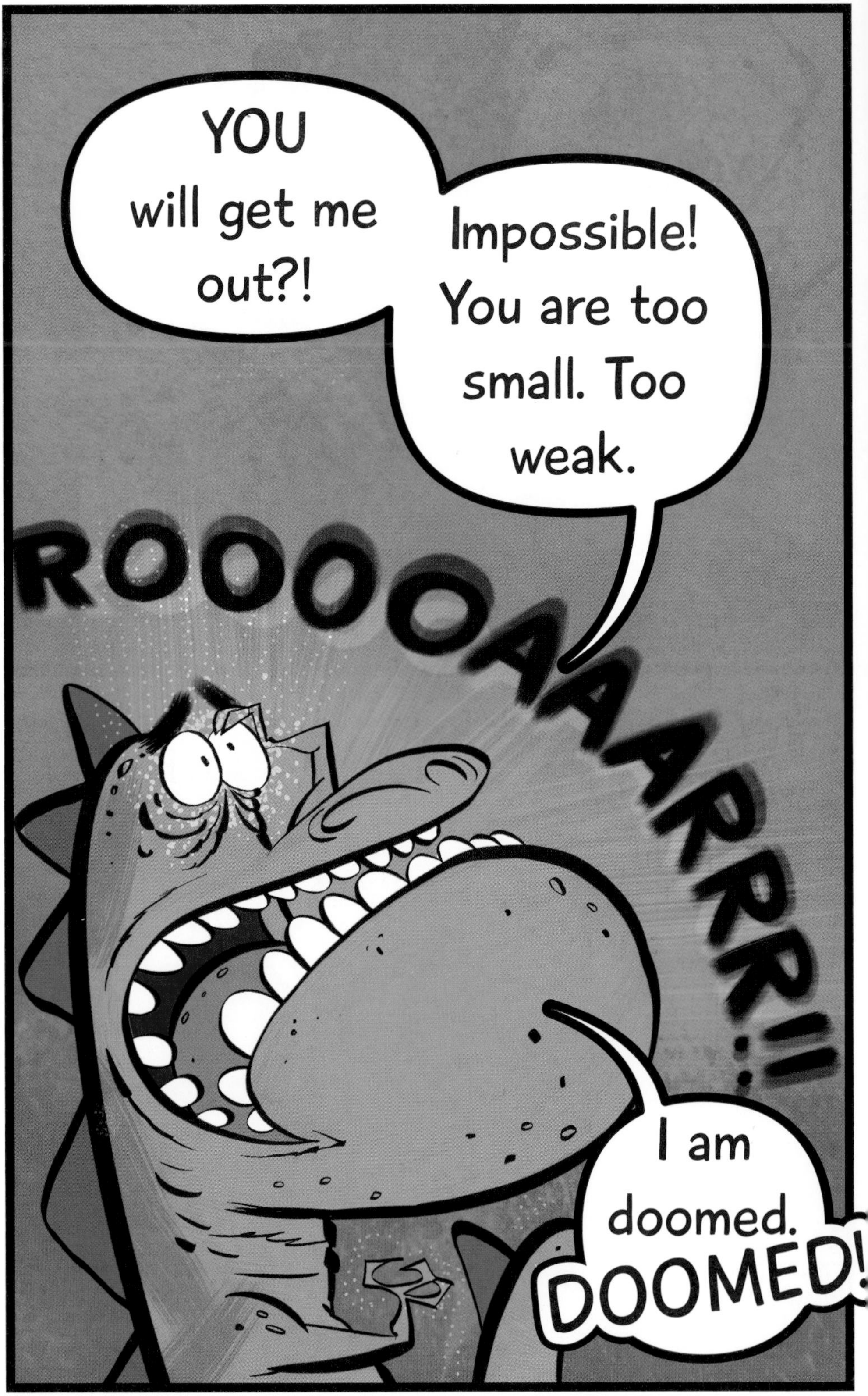
YOU will get me out?!
Impossible! You are too small. Too weak.
ROOOOAAAARRR!!!
I am doomed. DOOMED!

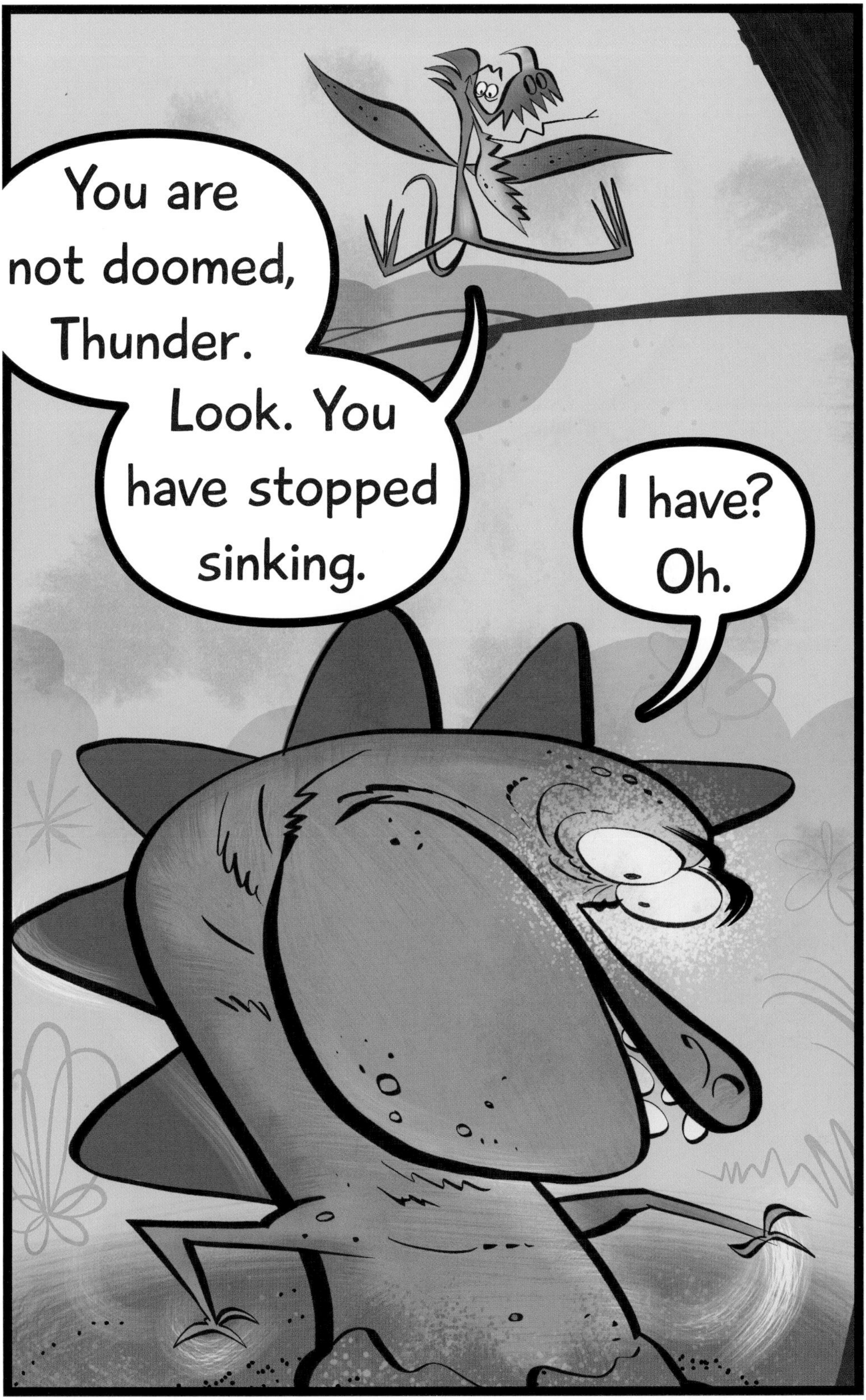
You are not doomed, Thunder.
Look. You have stopped sinking.
I have? Oh.

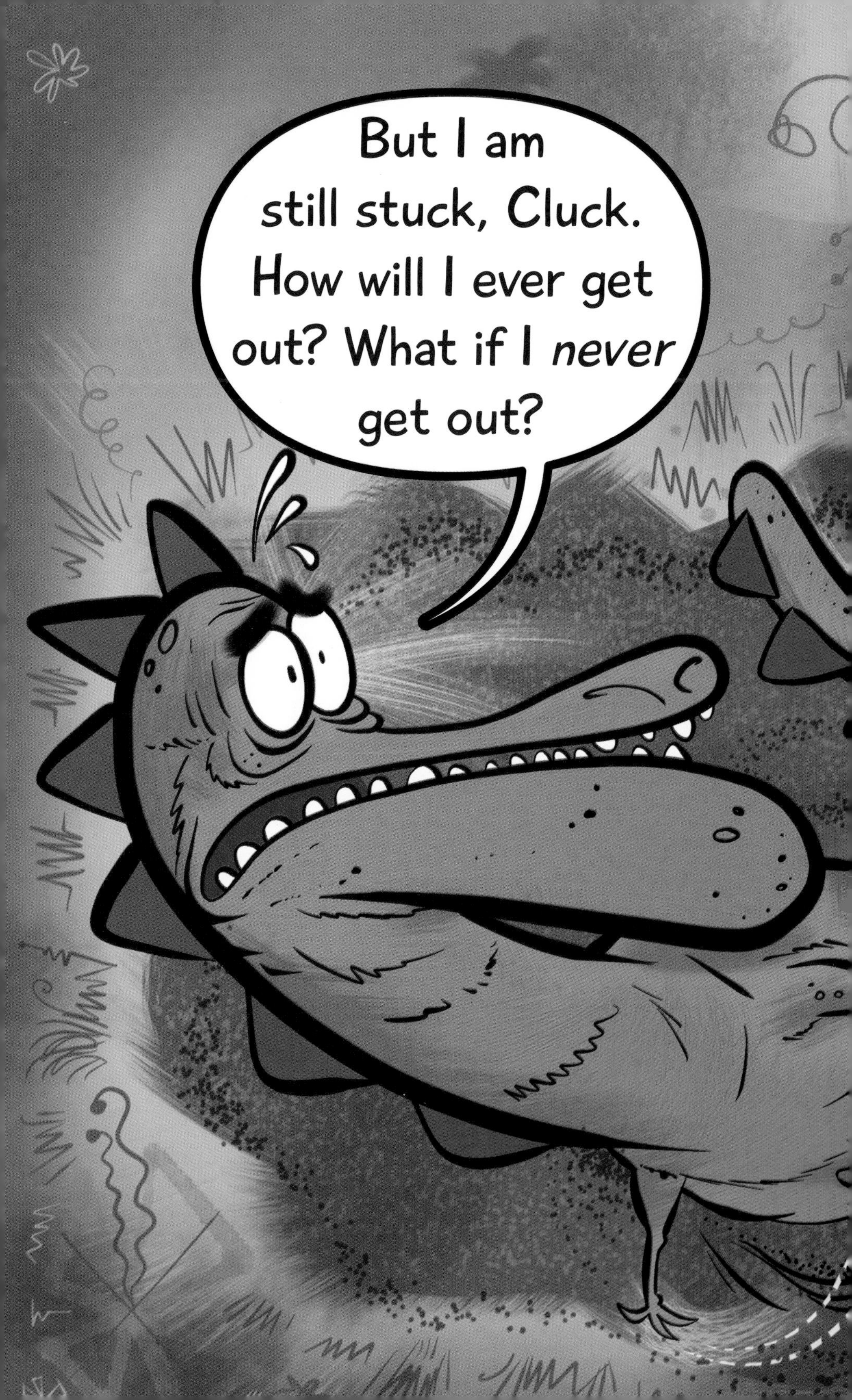
But I am still stuck, Cluck. How will I ever get out? What if I *never* get out?

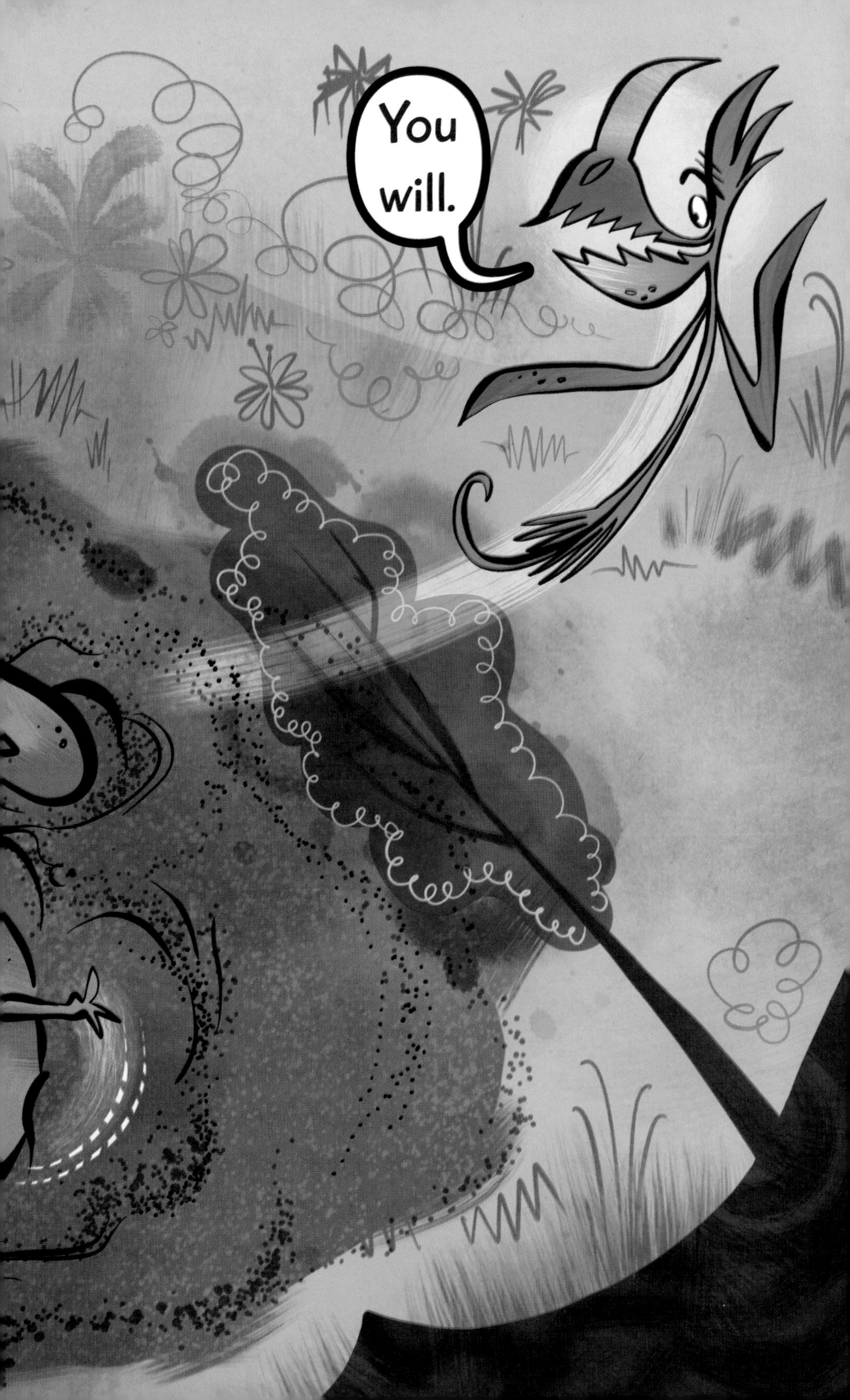
You will.

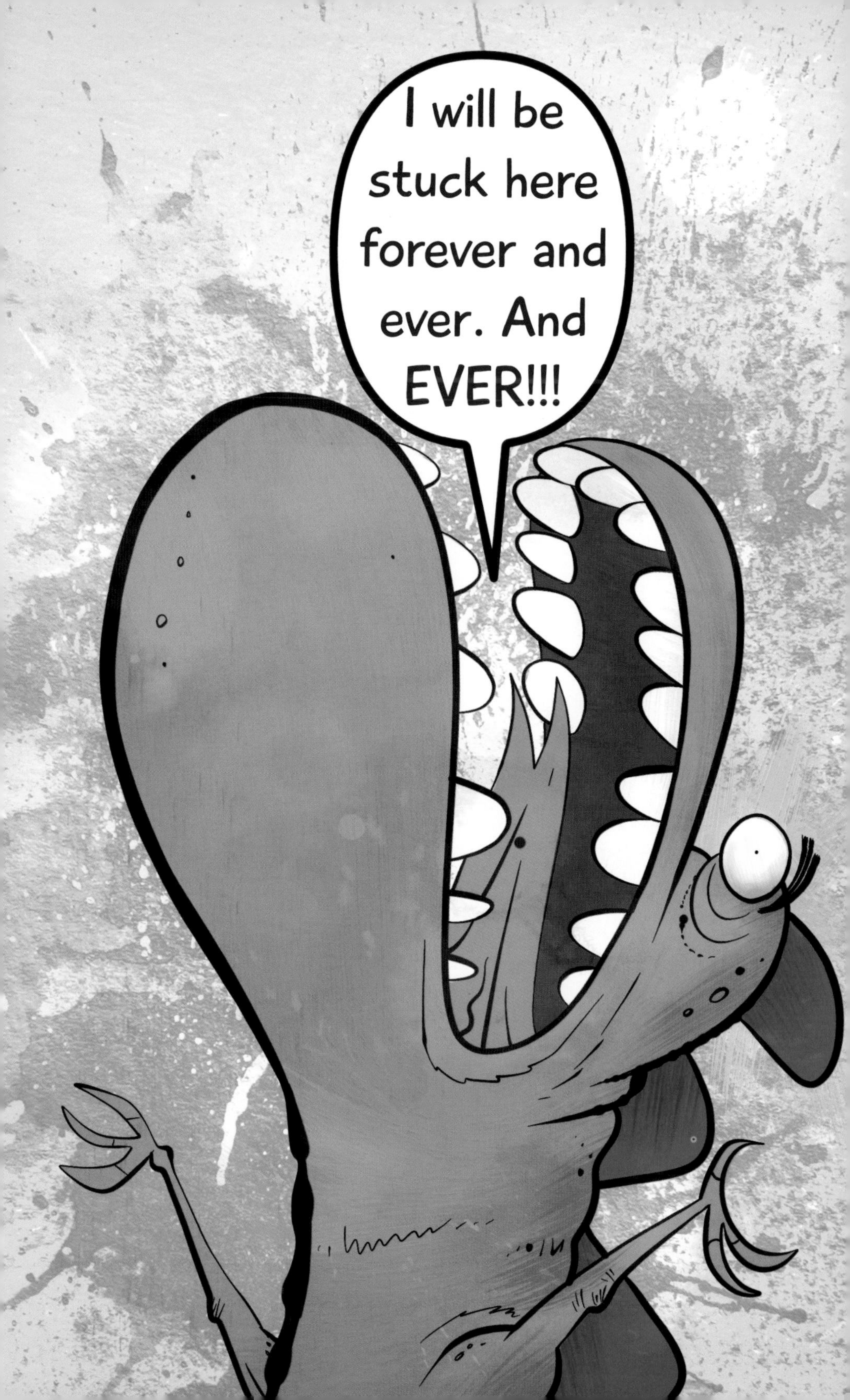
I will be stuck here forever and ever. And EVER!!!

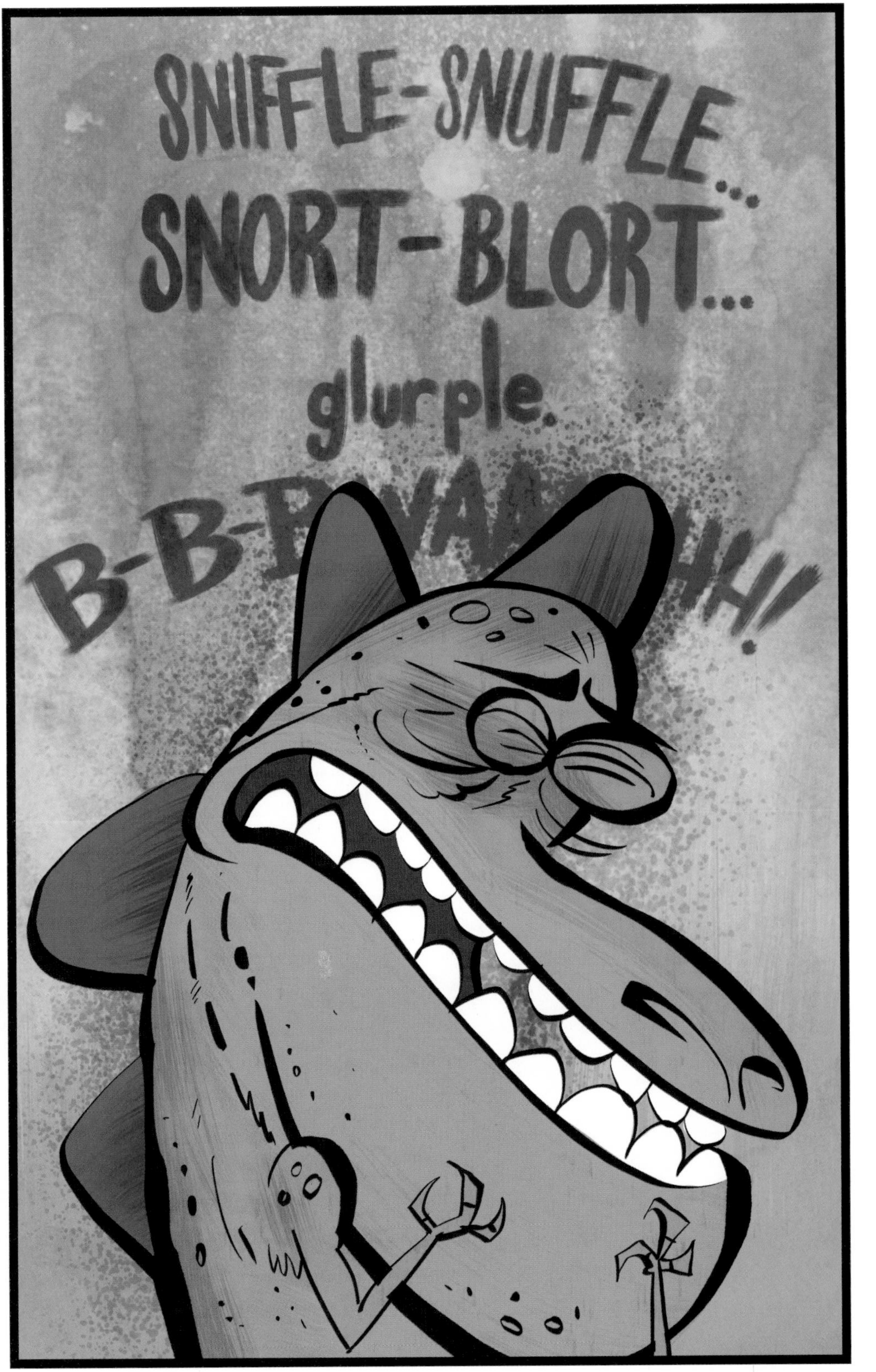
SNIFFLE-SNUFFLE...
SNORT-BLORT...
glurple.

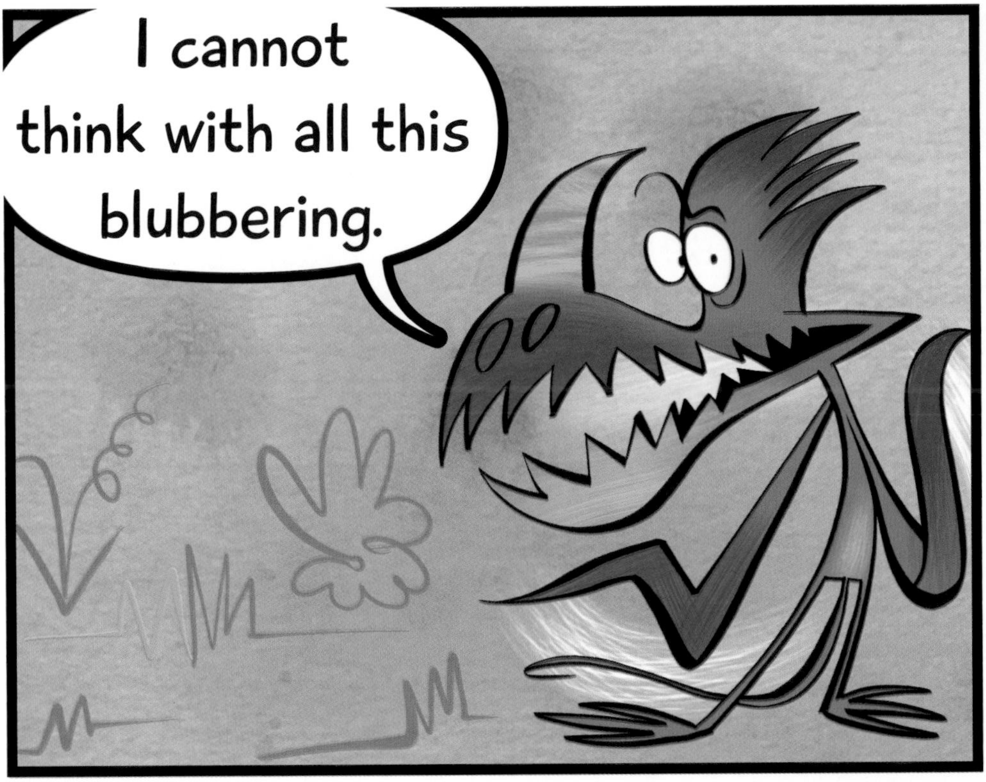
I cannot think with all this blubbering.

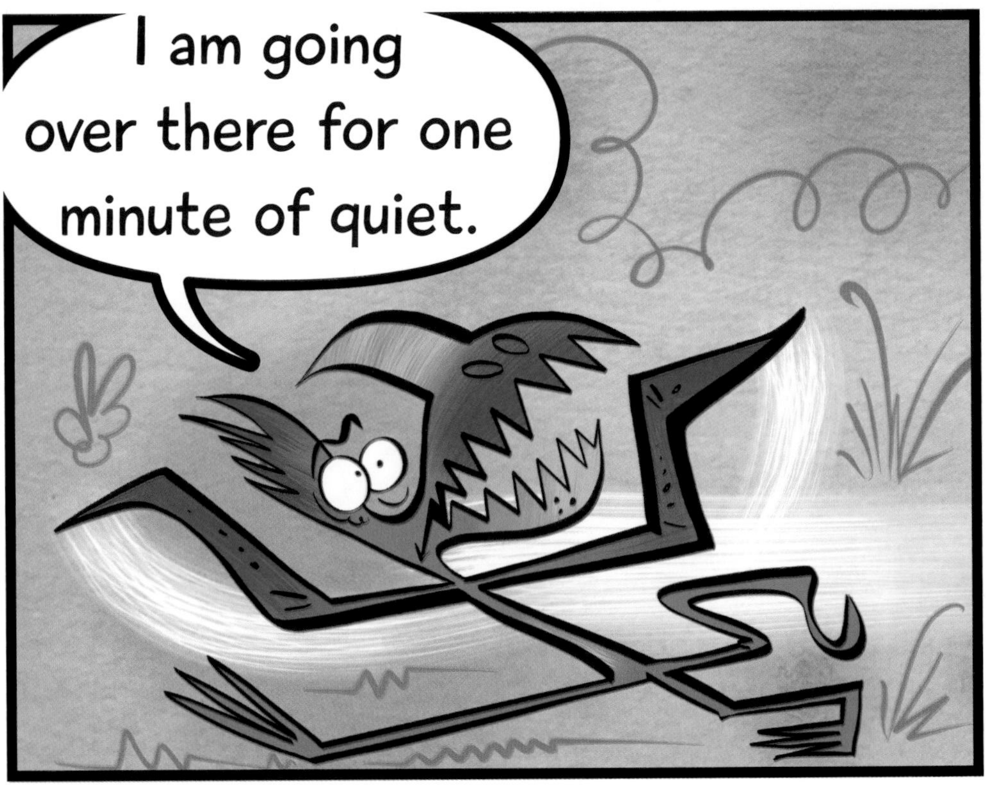
I am going over there for one minute of quiet.

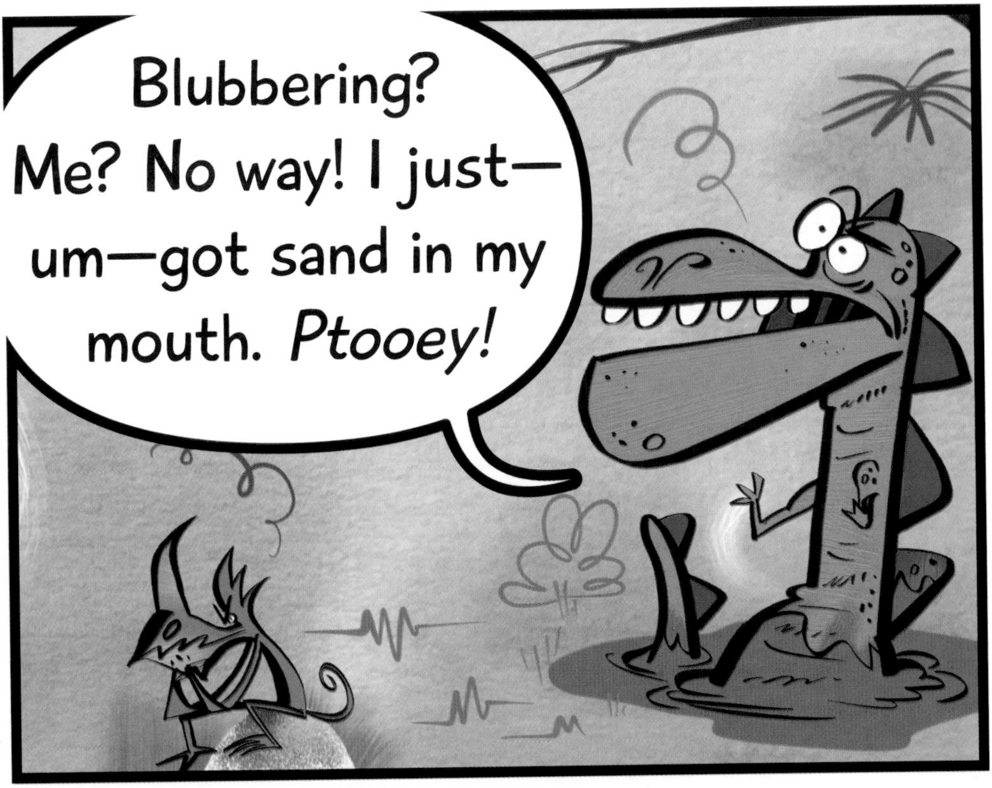
Blubbering? Me? No way! I just—um—got sand in my mouth. *Ptooey!*

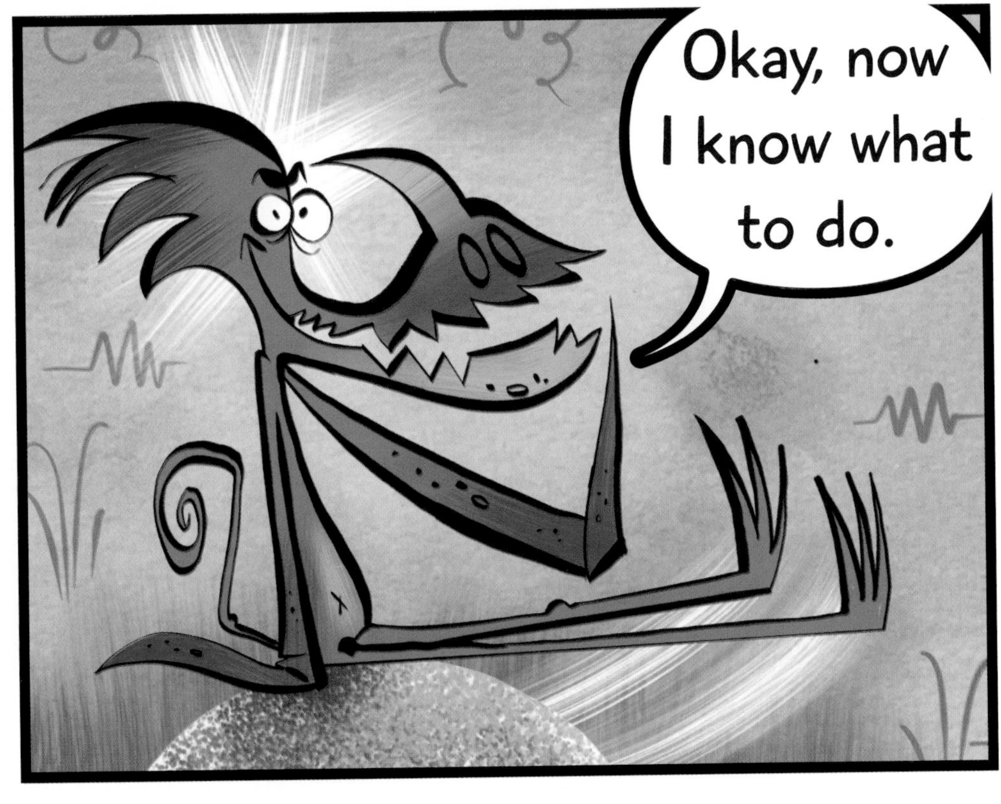
Okay, now I know what to do.

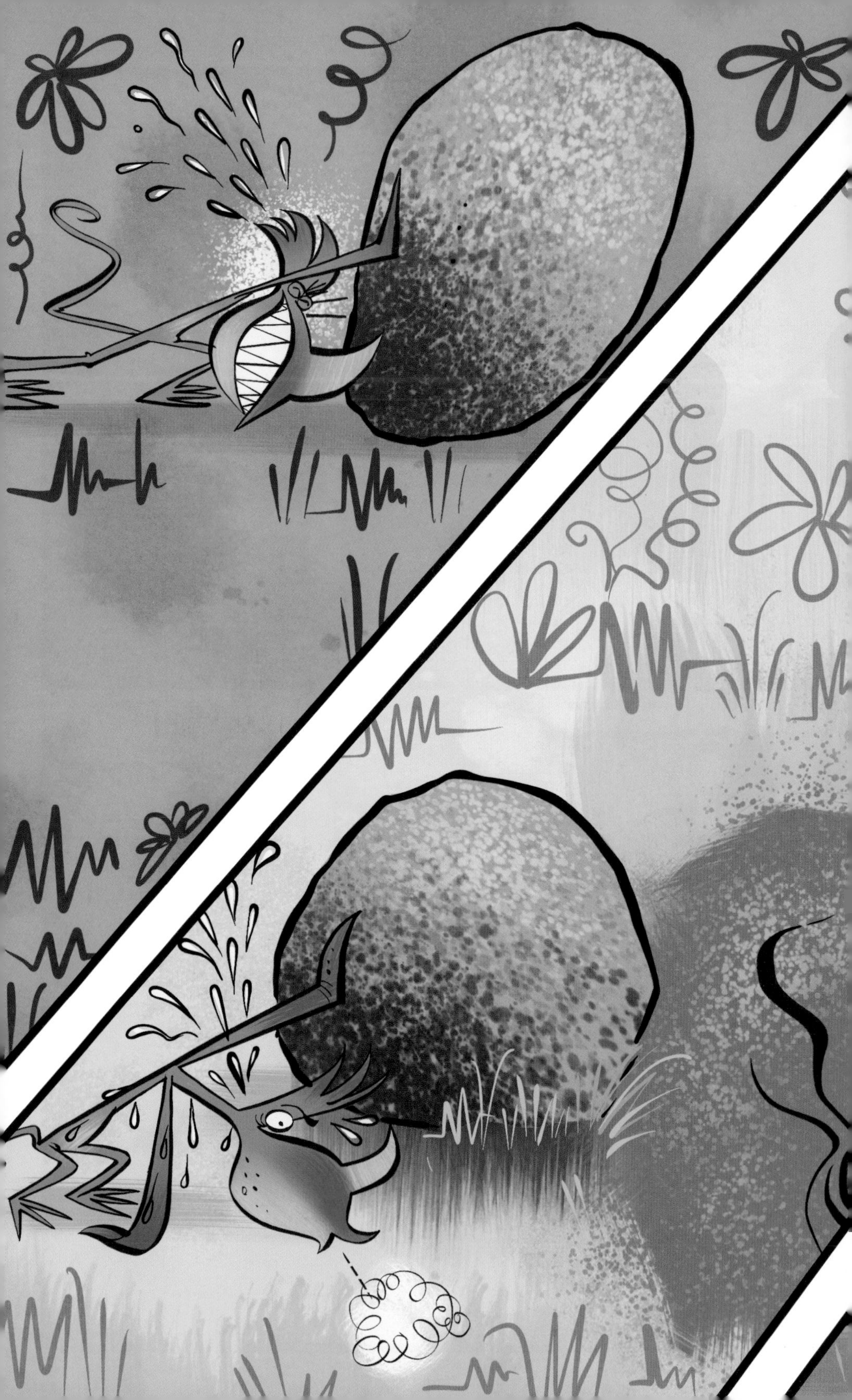

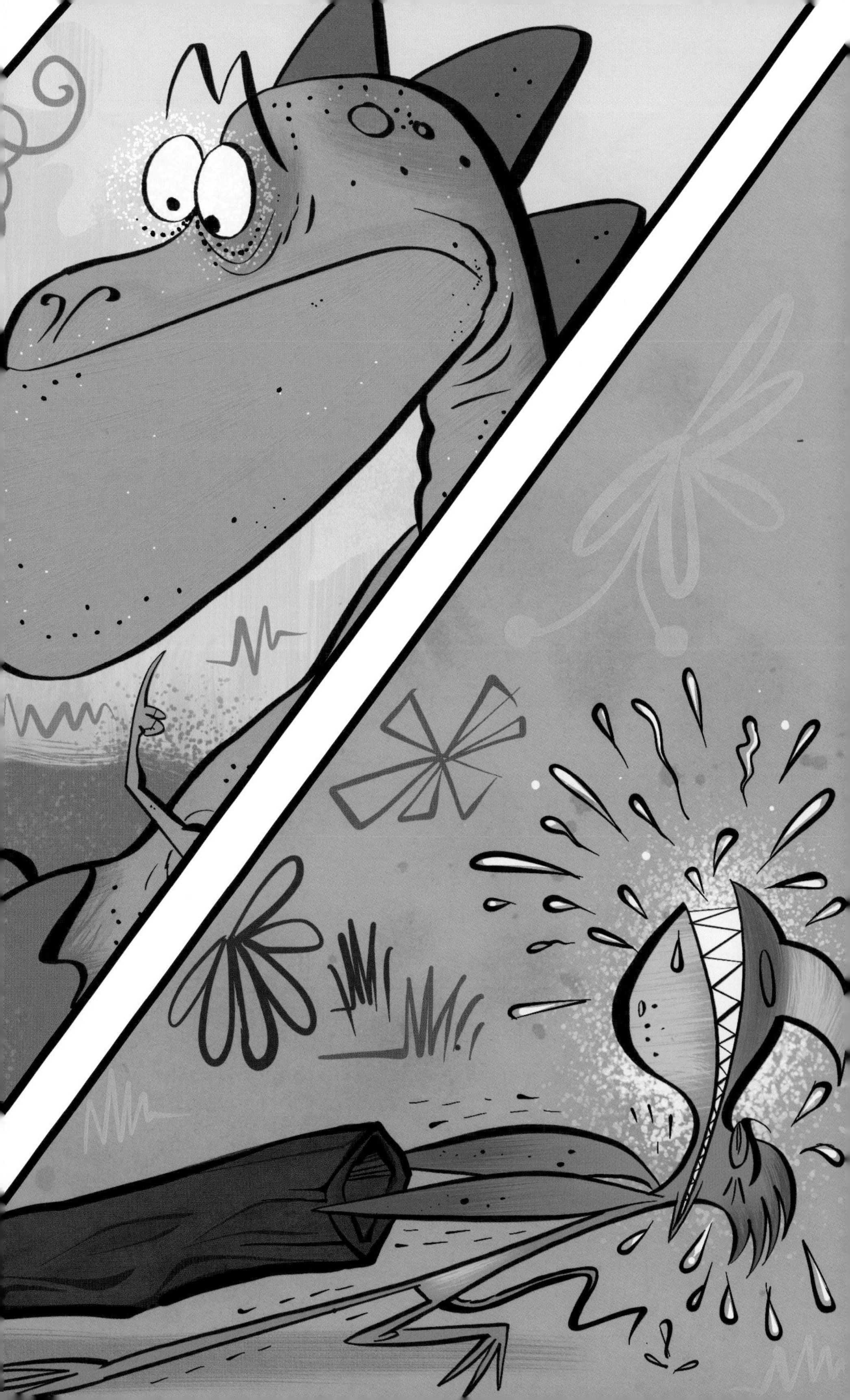

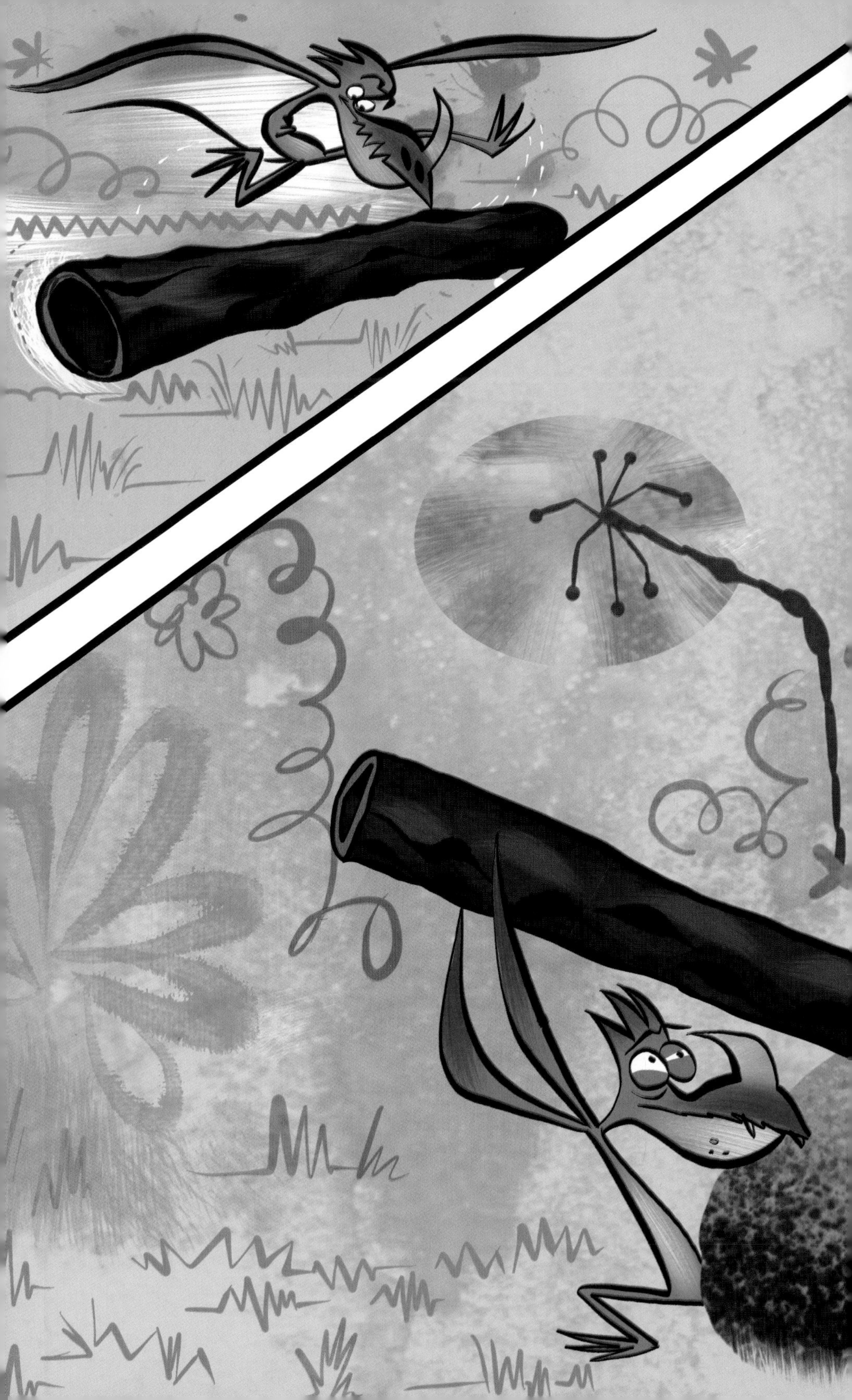

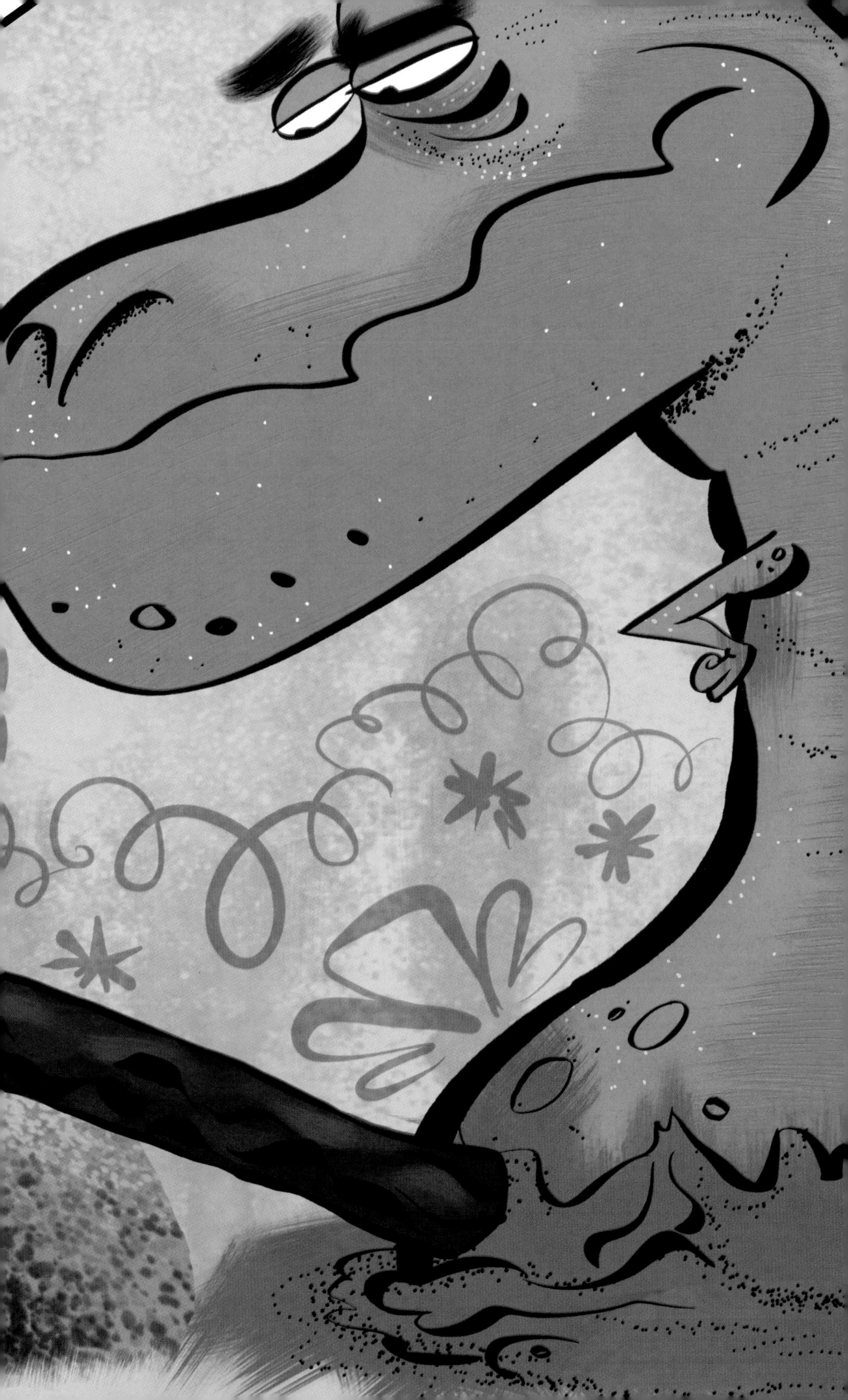

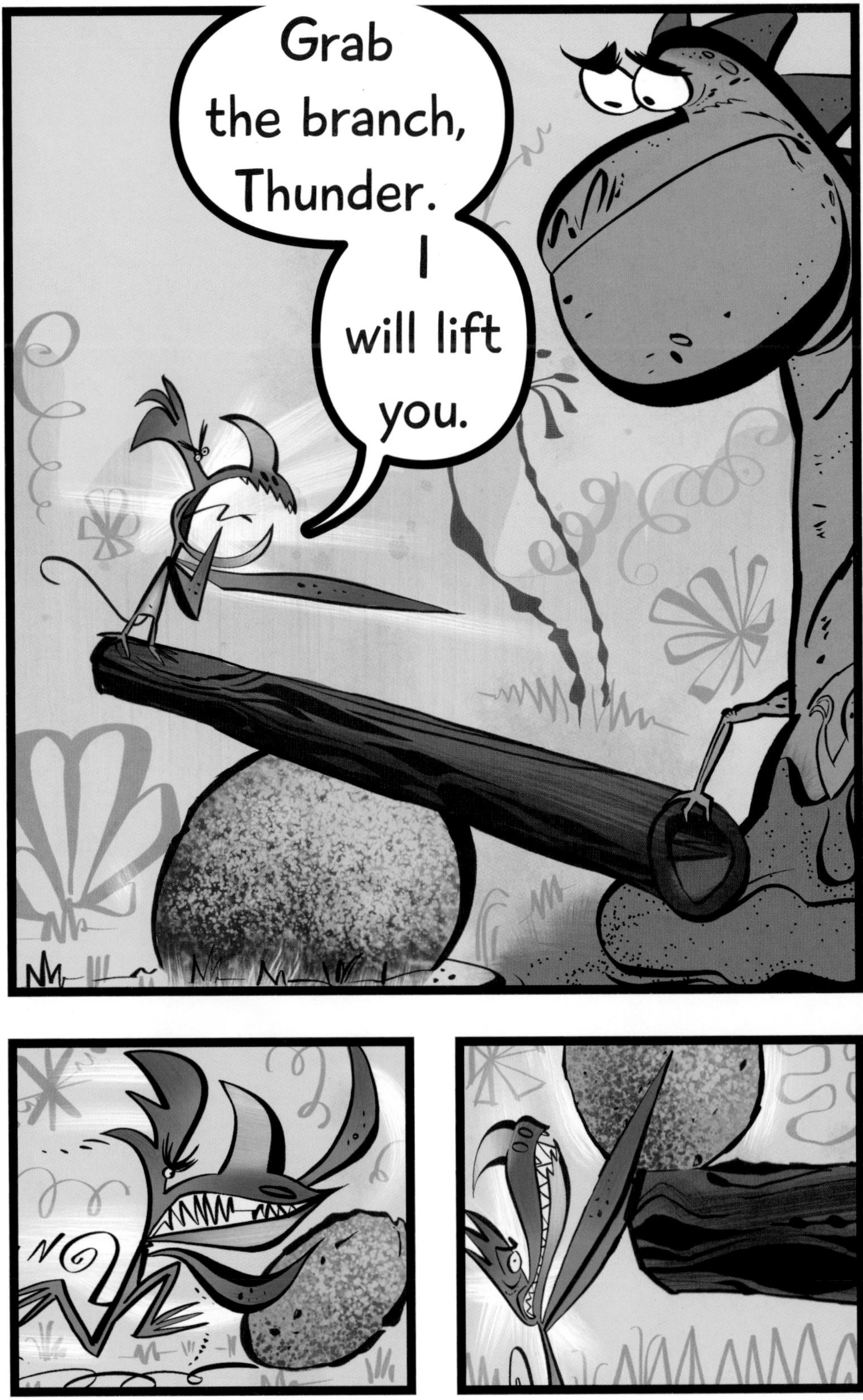
Grab the branch, Thunder.
I will lift you.

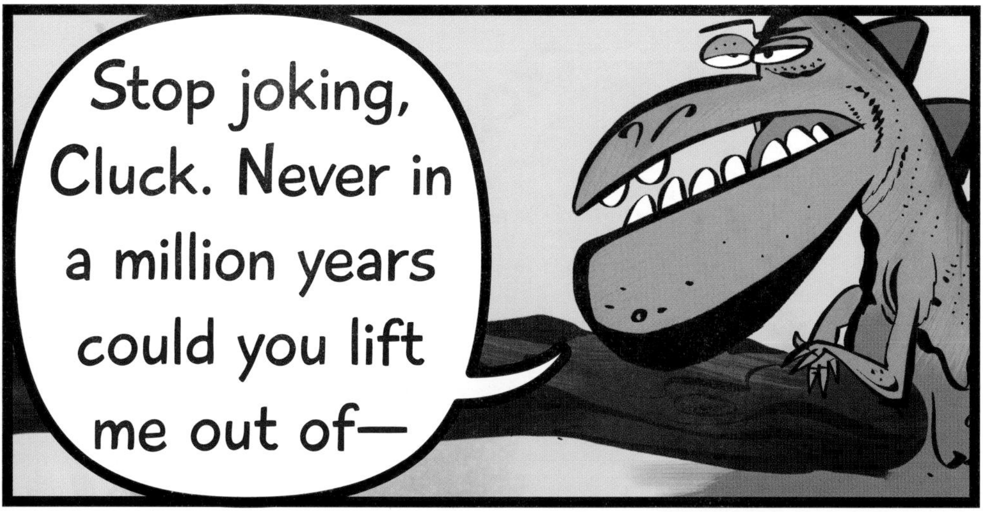
Stop joking, Cluck. Never in a million years could you lift me out of—

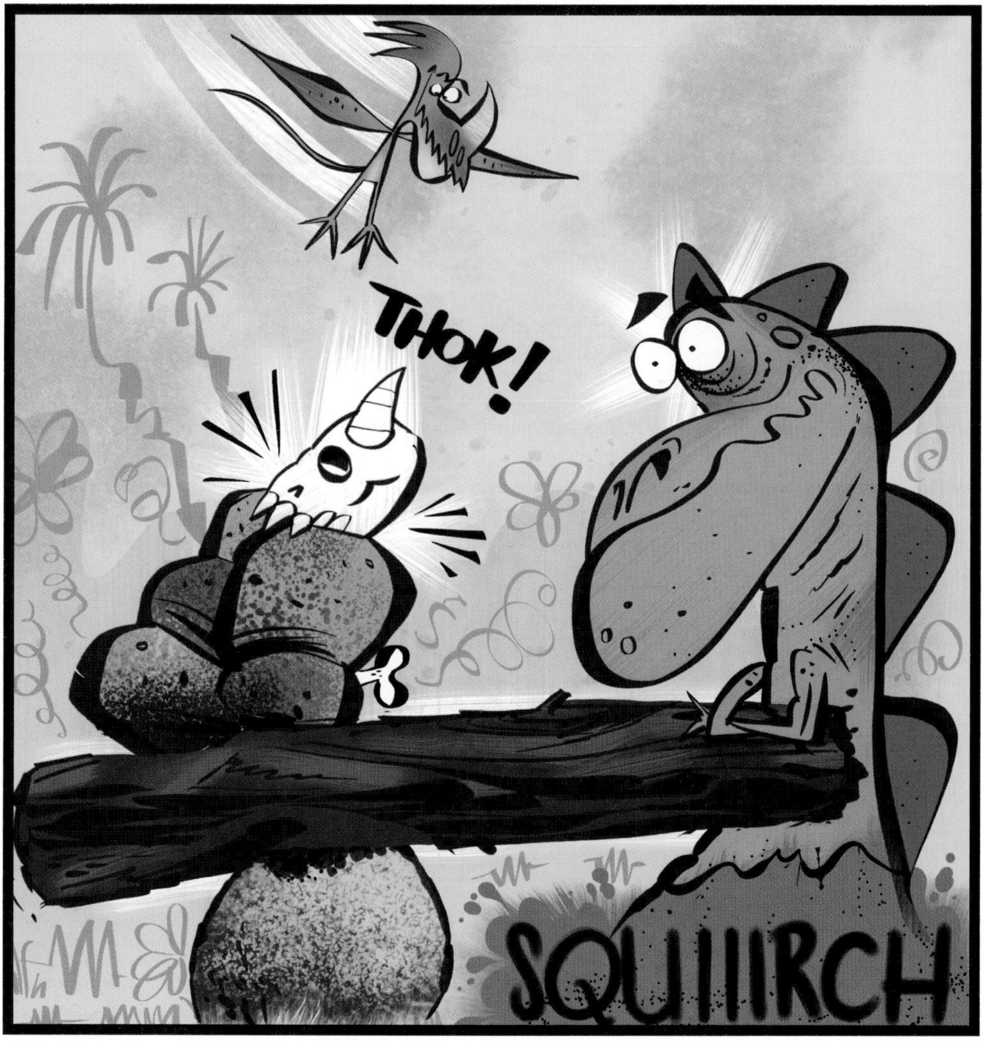
THOK!
SQUIIIRCH

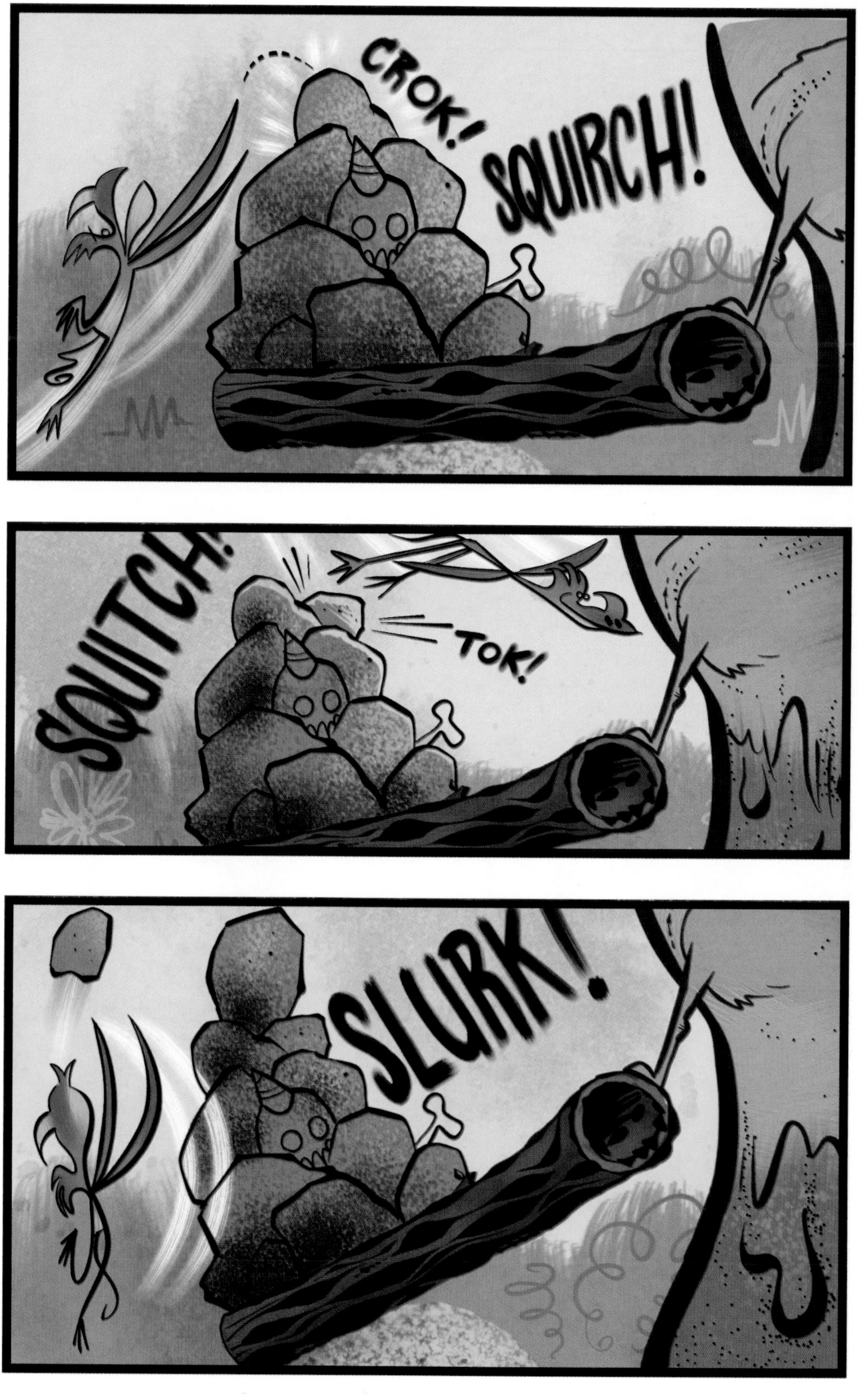
CROK!
SQUIRCH!
SQUITCH!
TOK!
SLURK!

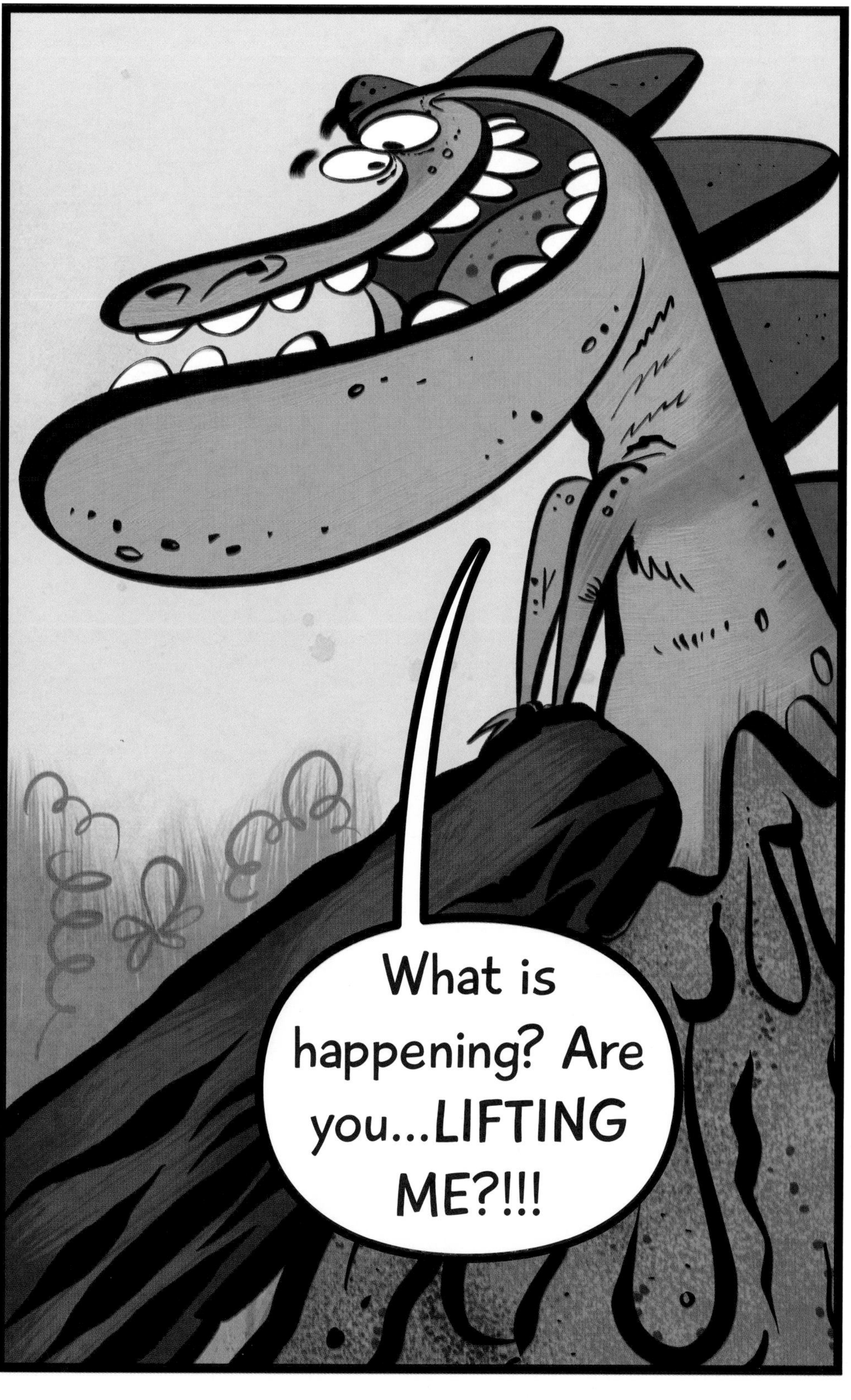
What is happening? Are you...LIFTING ME?!!!

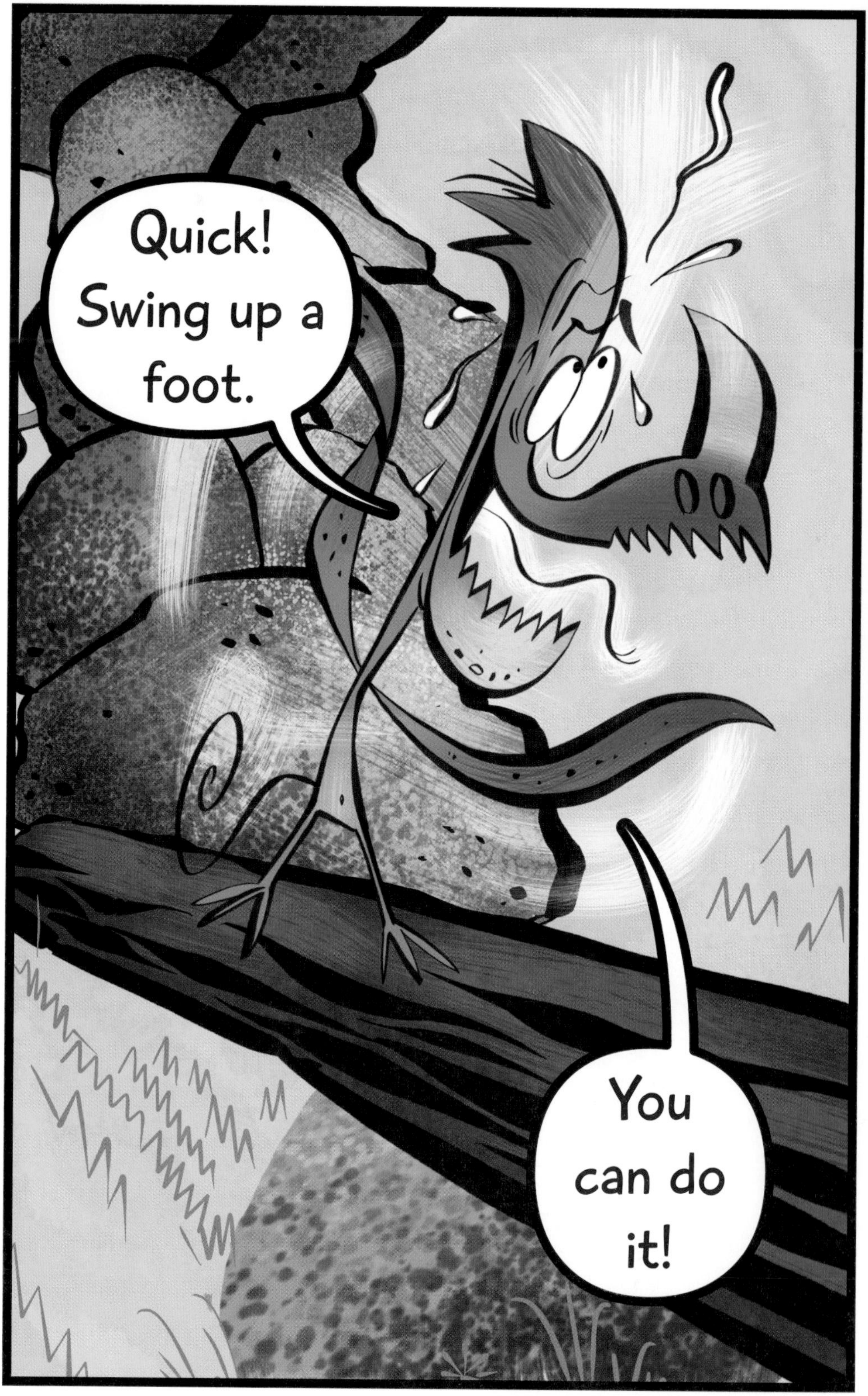
Quick! Swing up a foot.
You can do it!

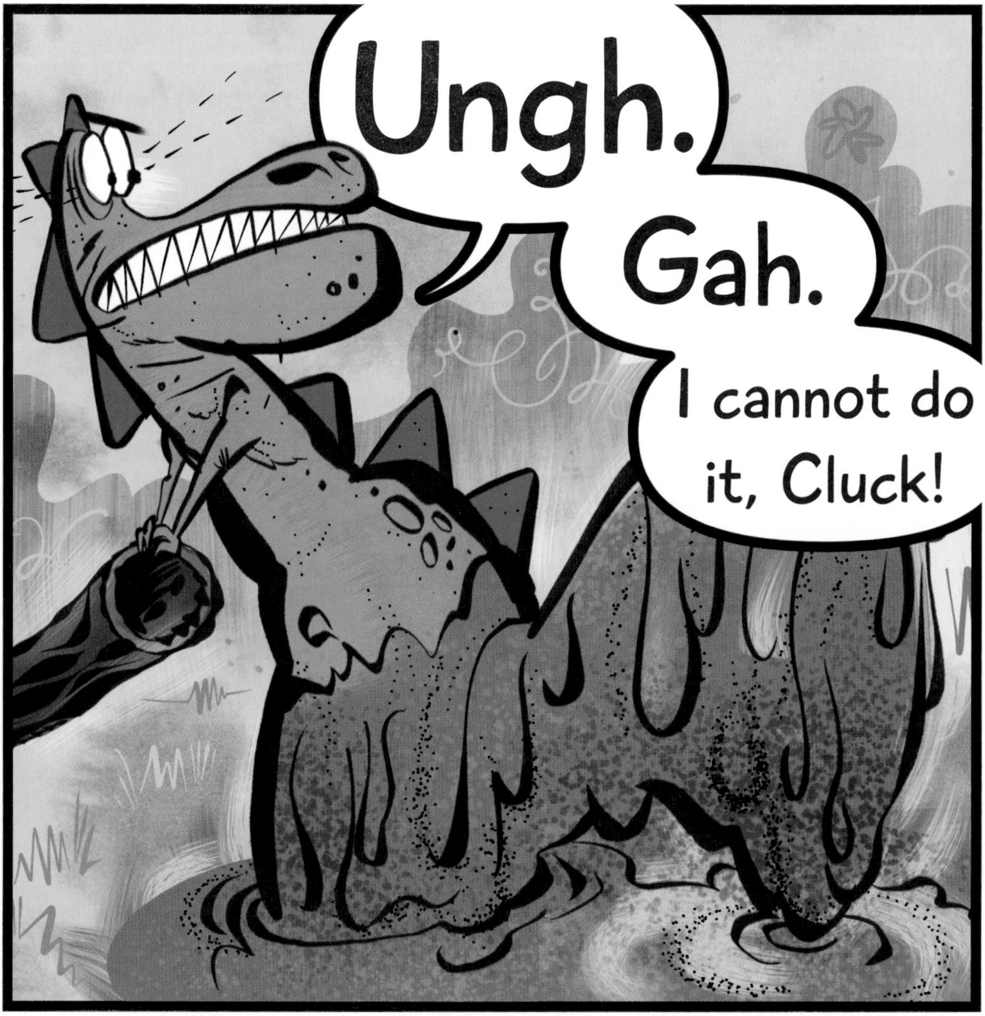
Ungh.
Gah.
I cannot do it, Cluck!

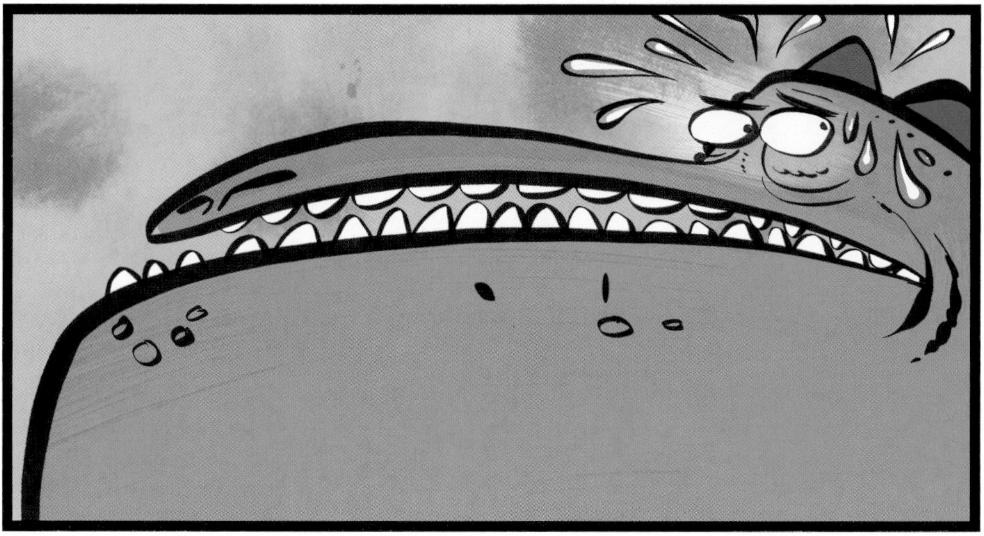

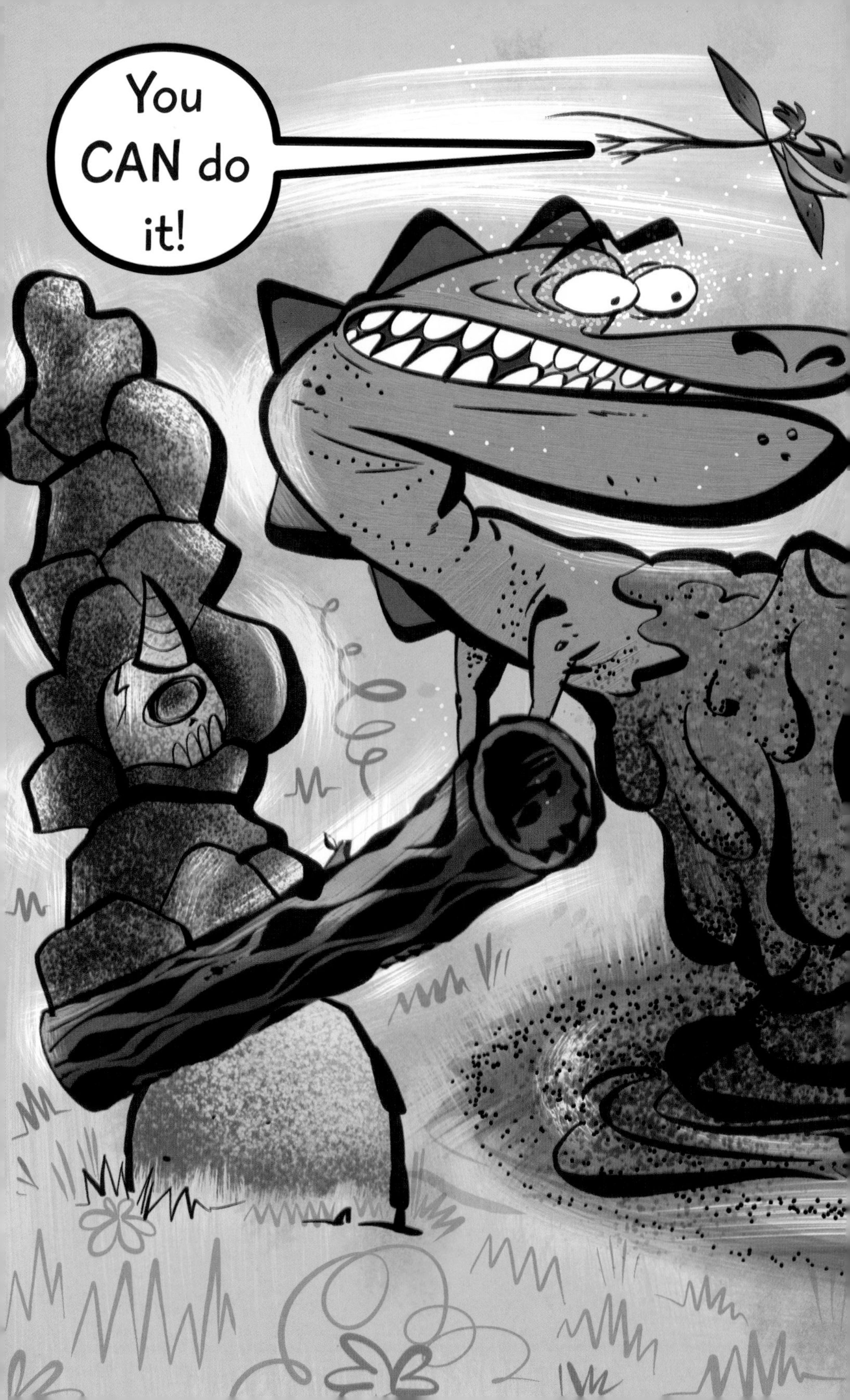
You CAN do it!

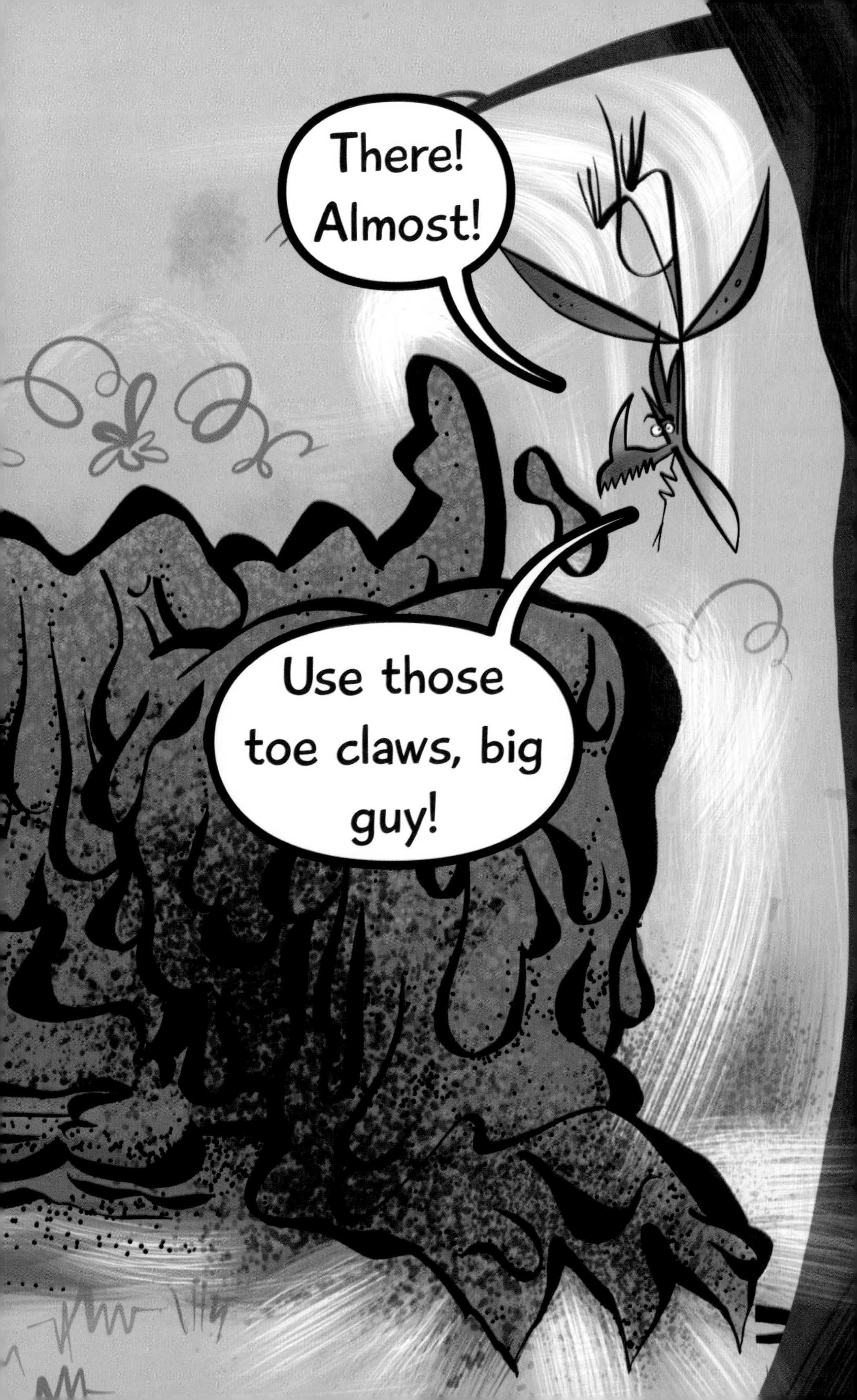
There! Almost!
Use those toe claws, big guy!

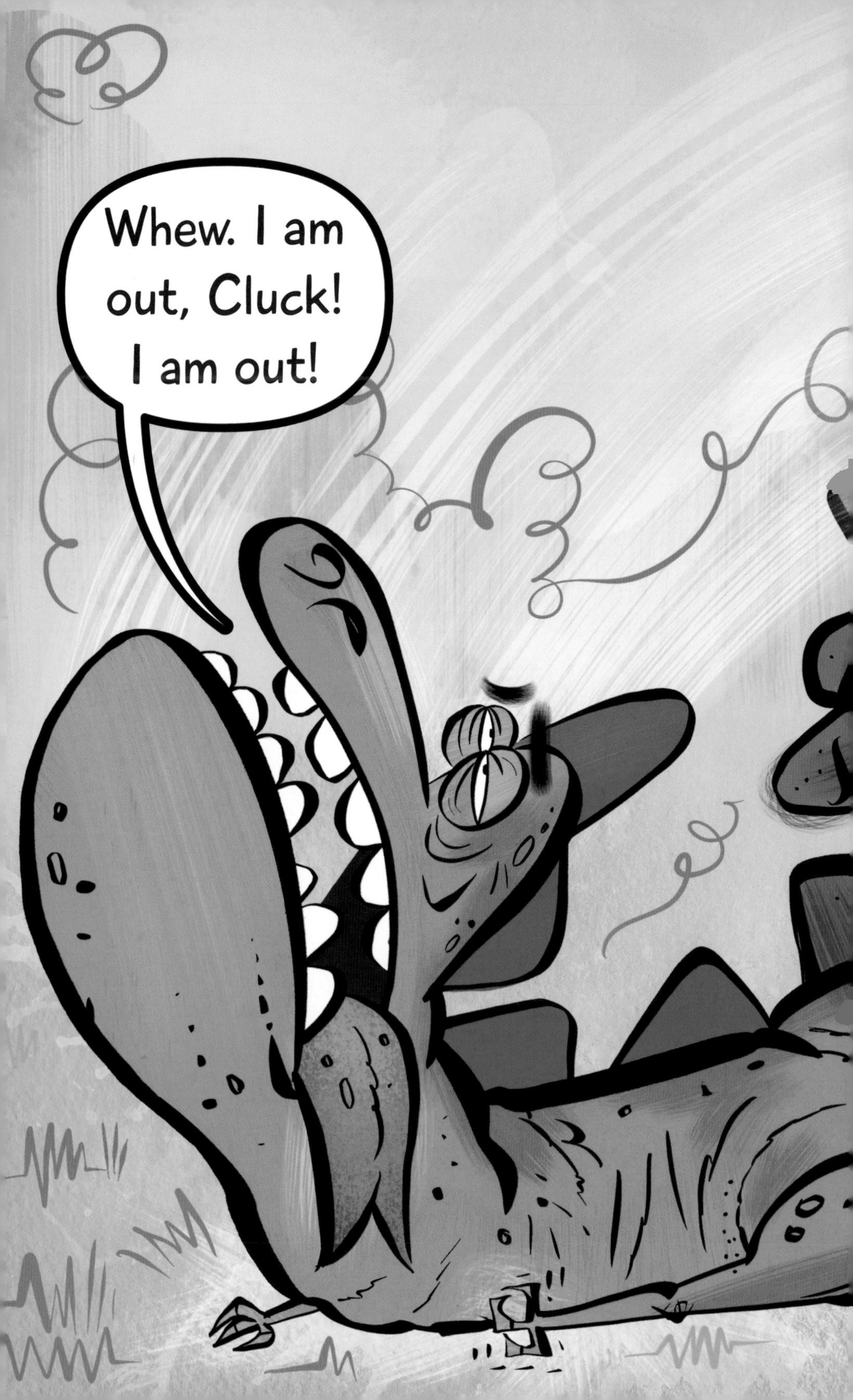
Whew. I am out, Cluck! I am out!

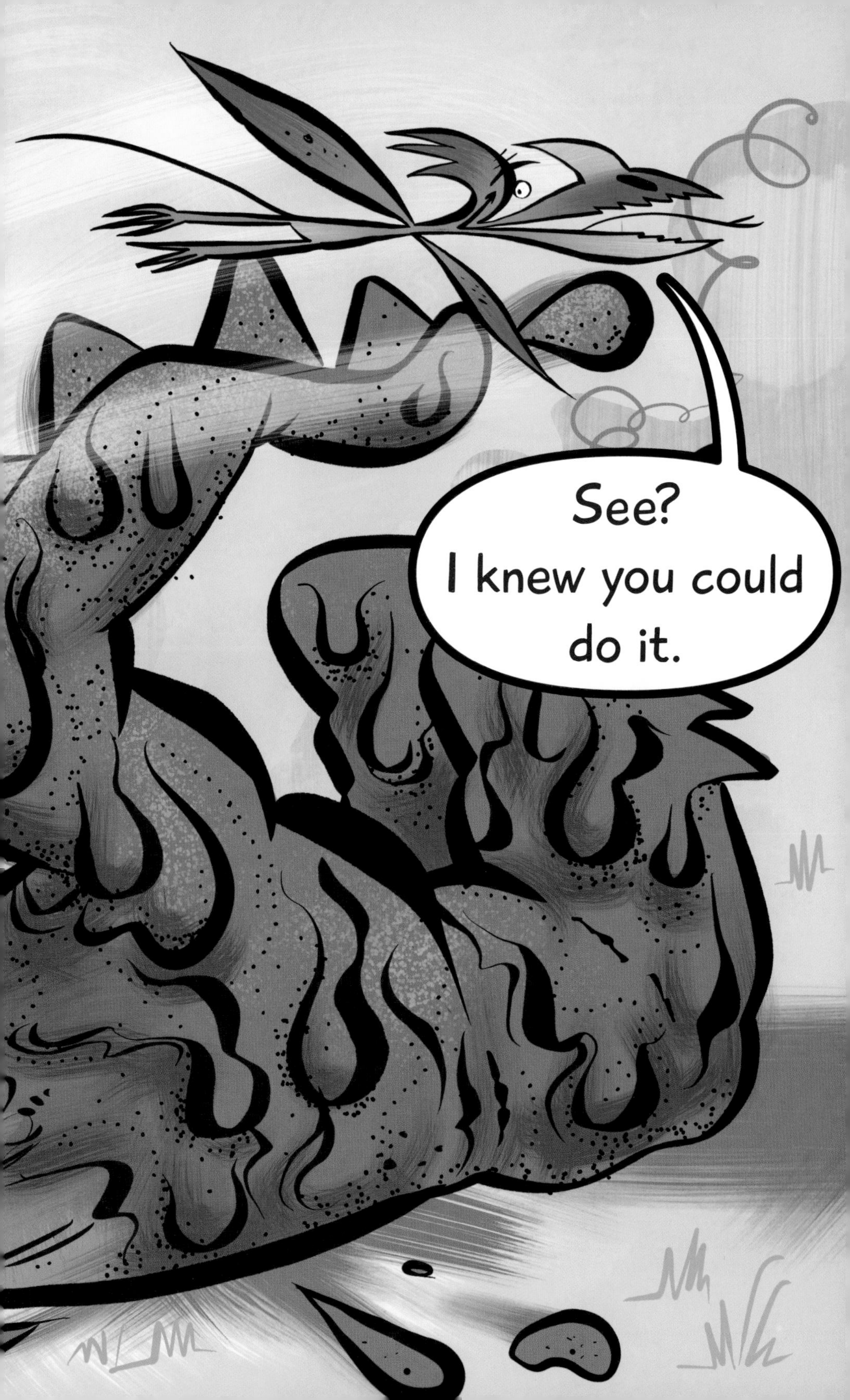
See?
I knew you could do it.

Tell me, my smart friend, what do you call that lifter-thingy you made?
Um... a Lifter-Thingy.

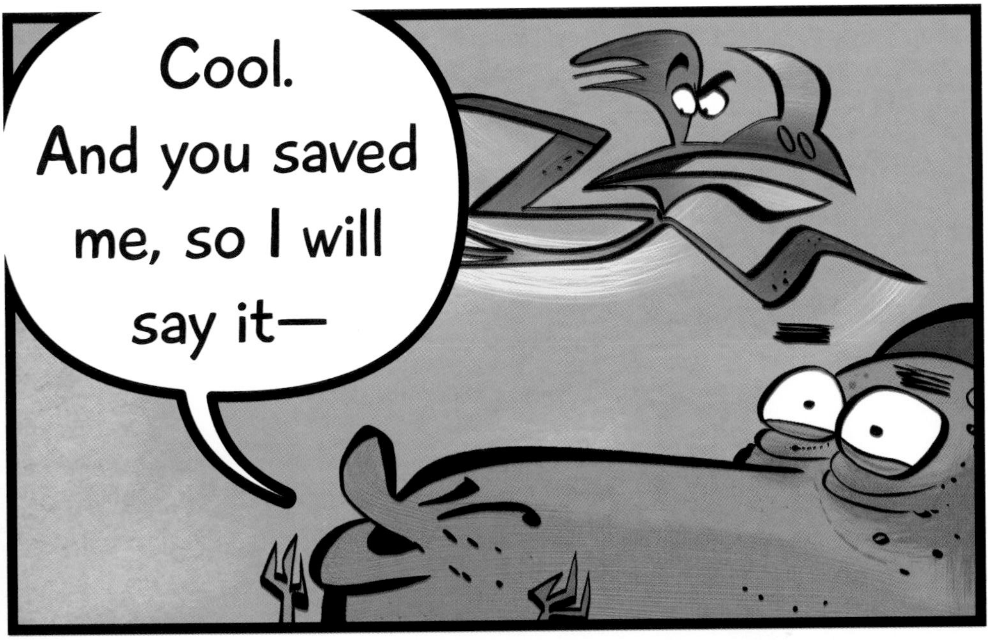
Cool.
And you saved me, so I will say it—

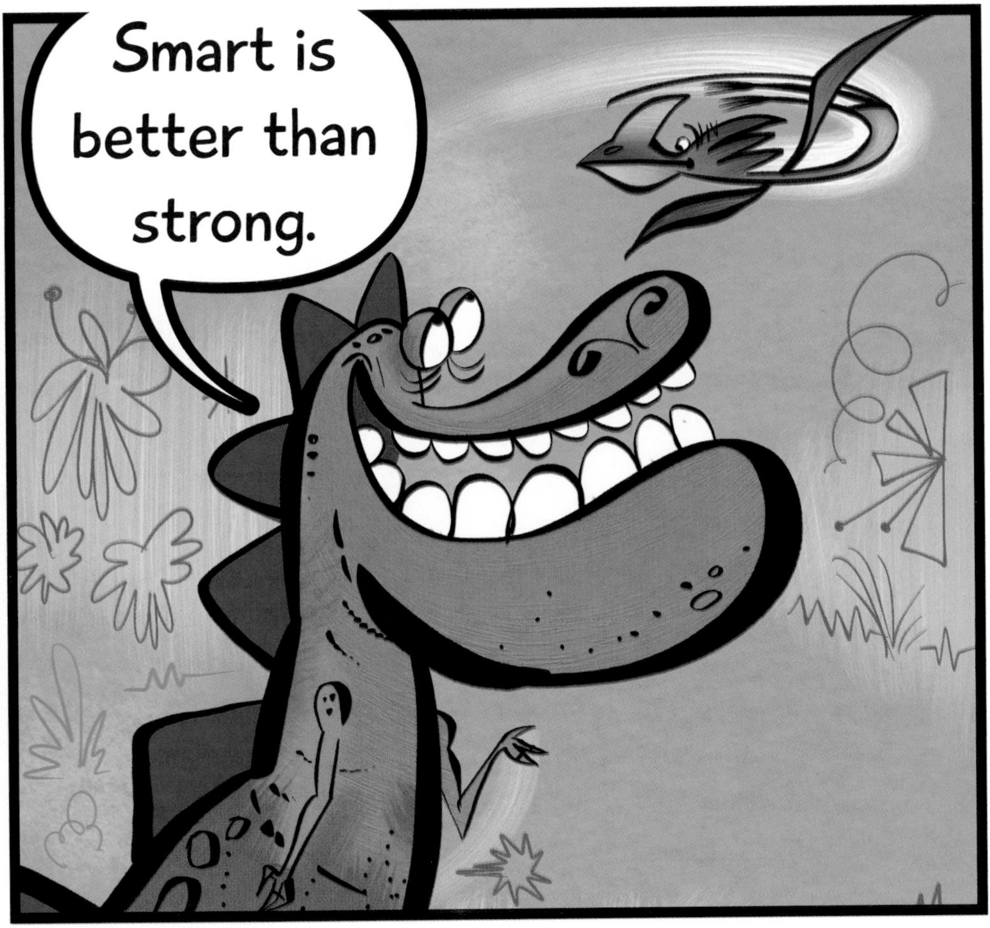
Smart is better than strong.

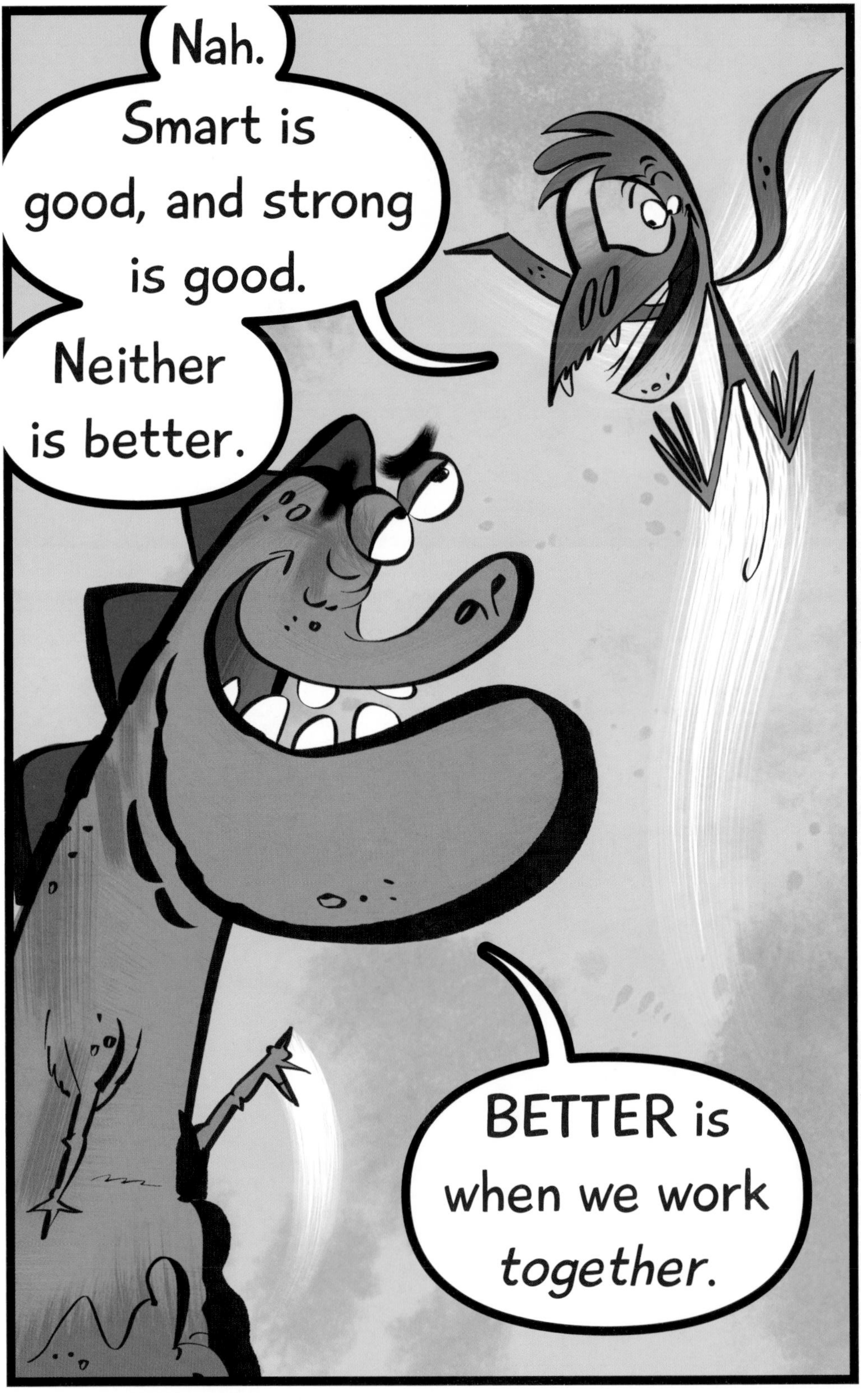
Nah.
Smart is good, and strong is good.
Neither is better.
BETTER is when we work *together*.

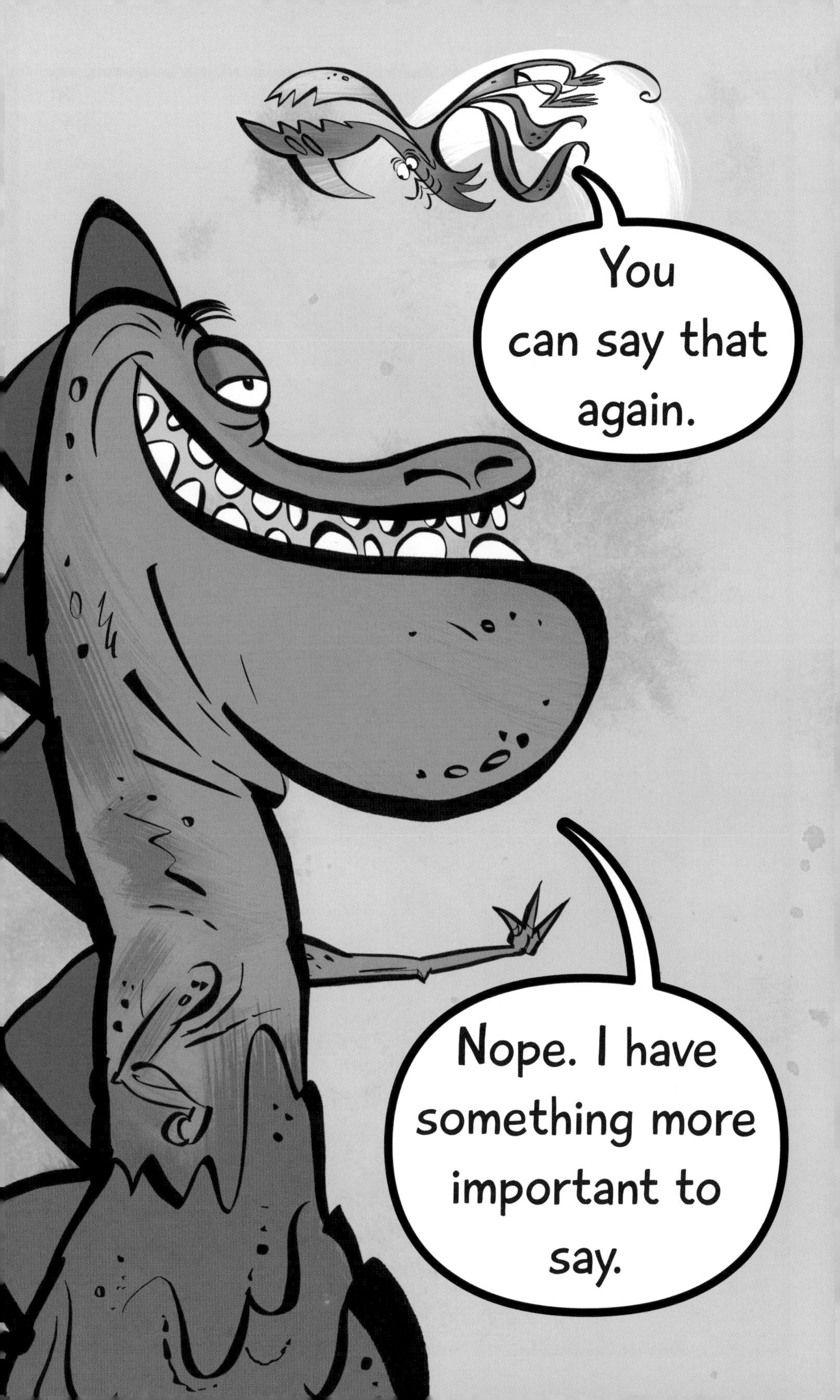
You can say that again.
Nope. I have something more important to say.

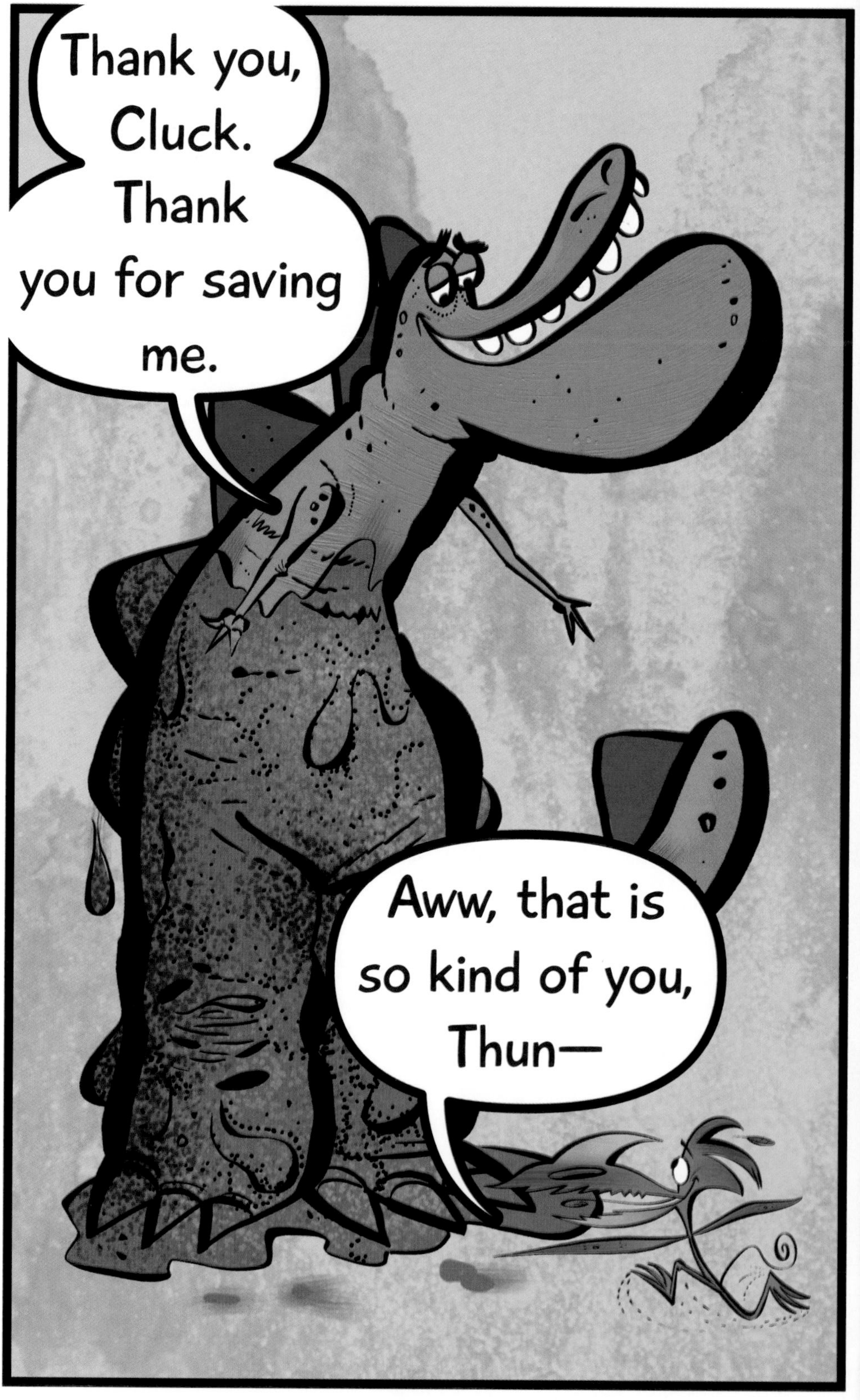
Thank you, Cluck. Thank you for saving me.
Aww, that is so kind of you, Thun—

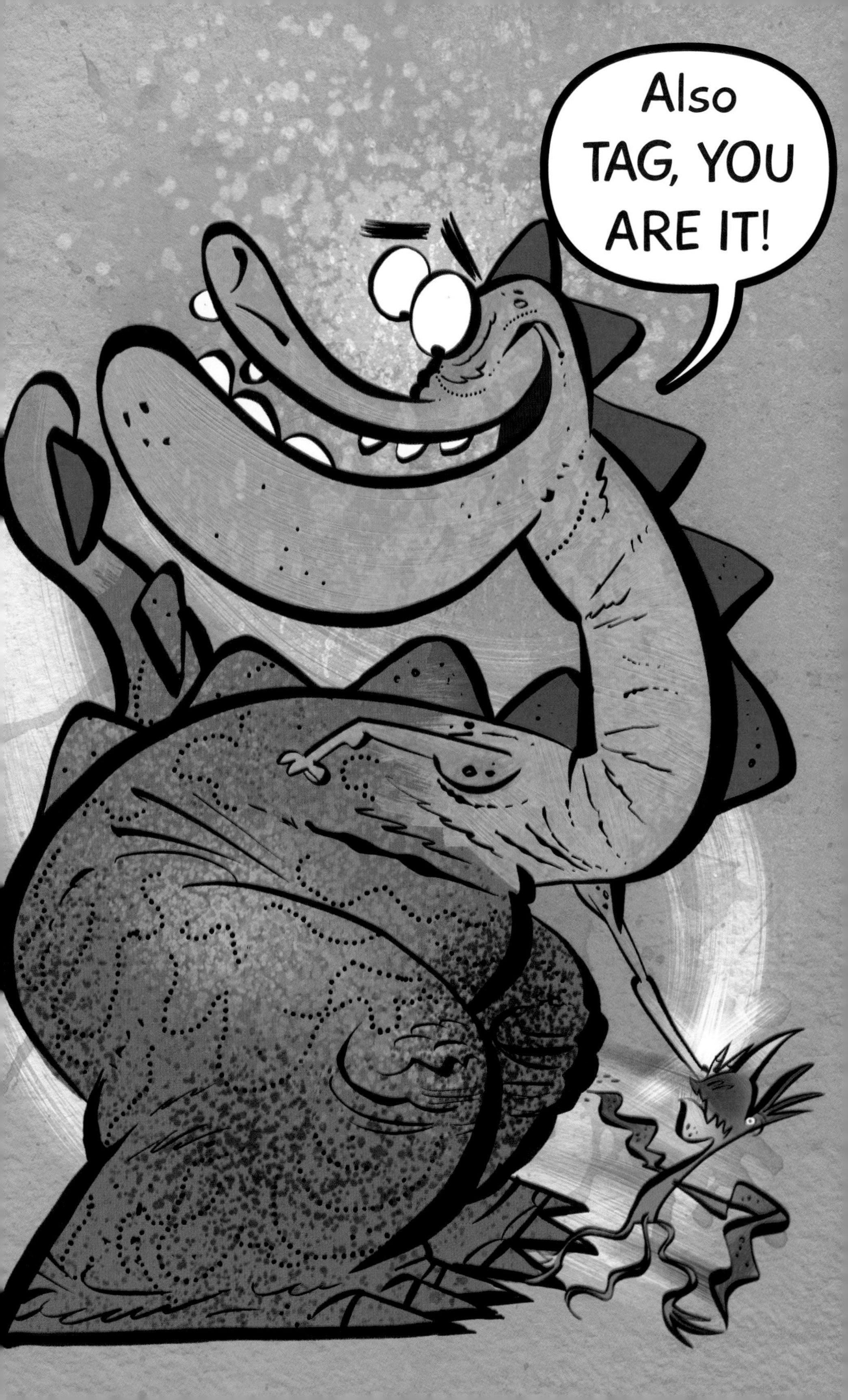
Also TAG, YOU ARE IT!

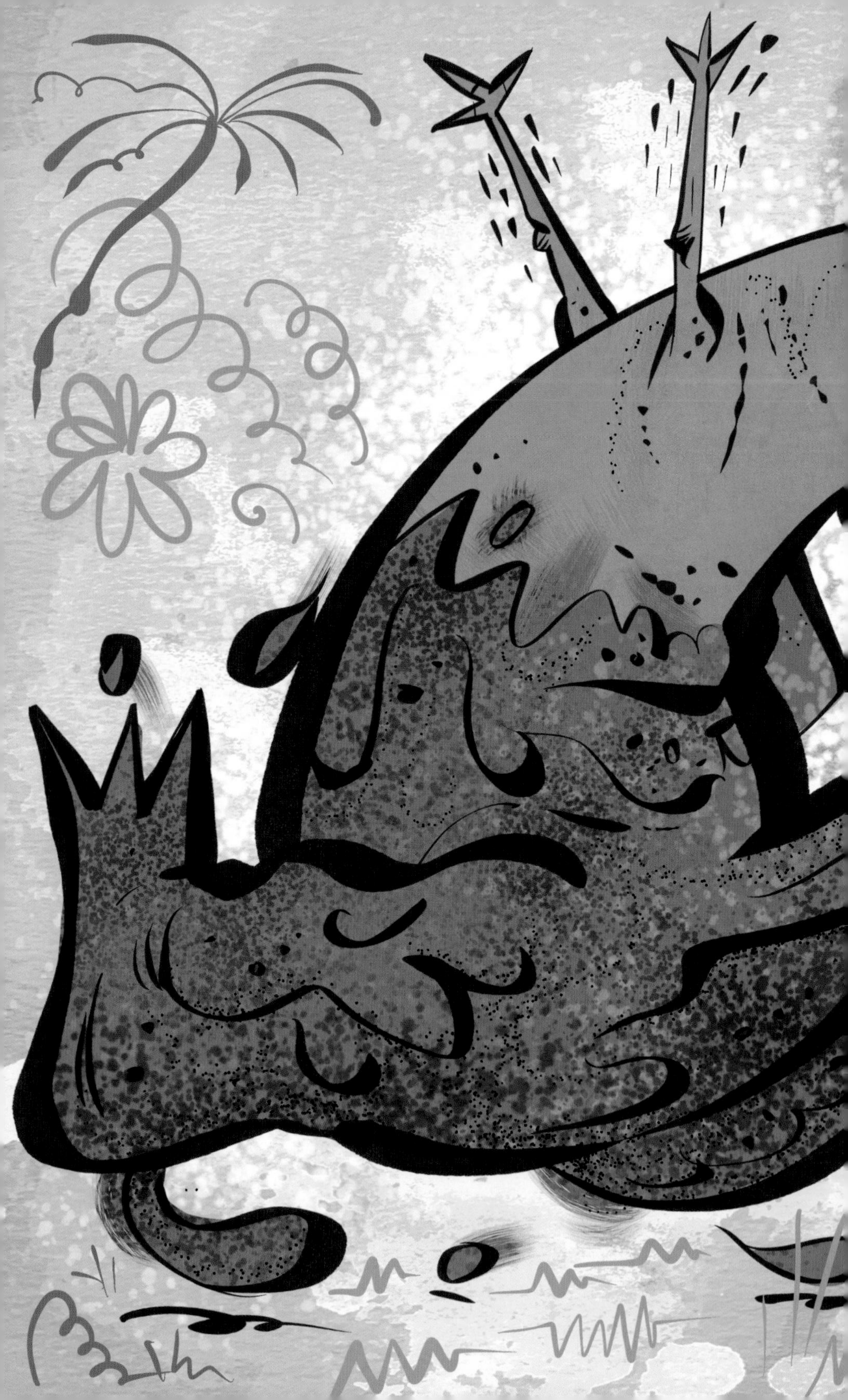

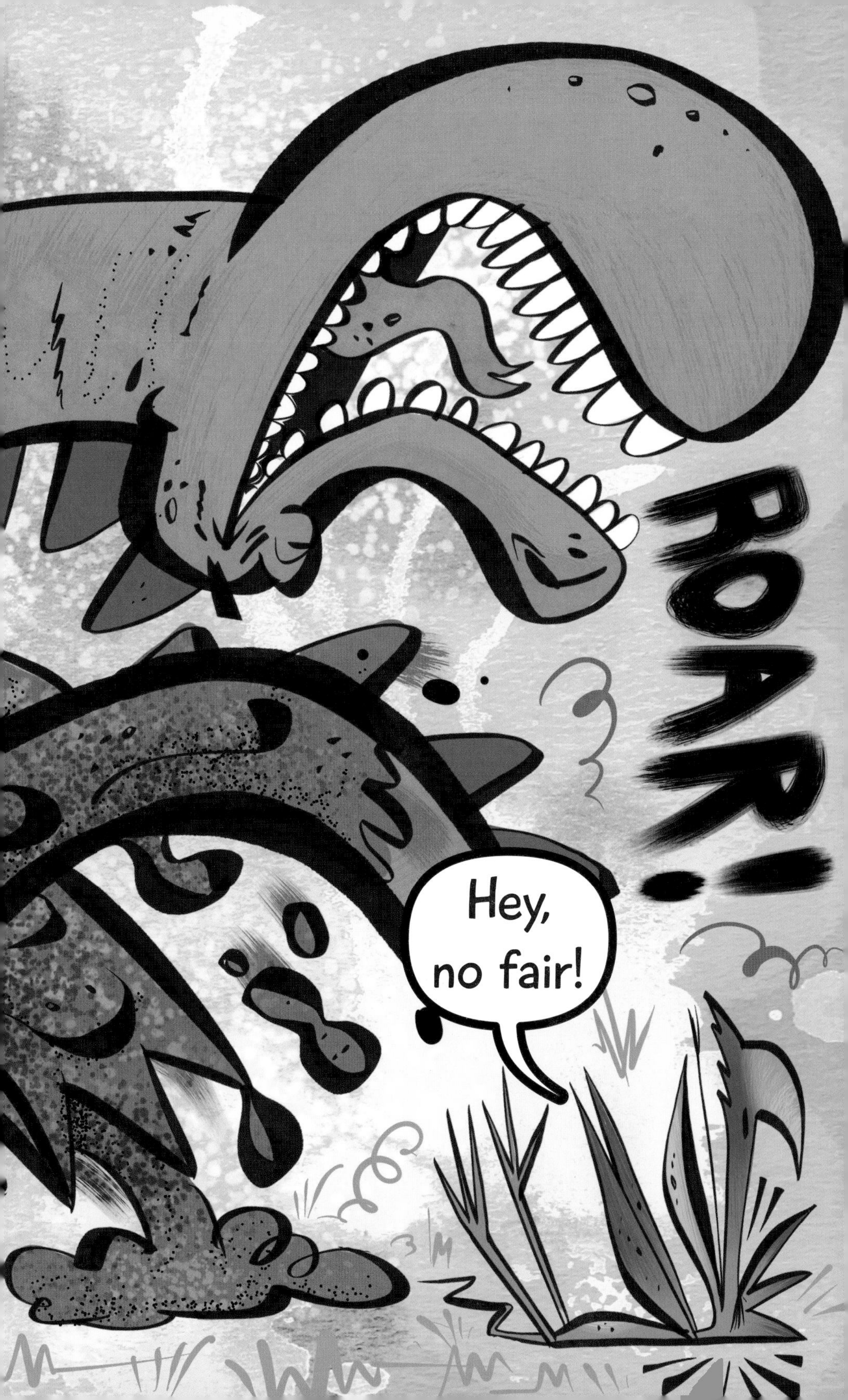
ROAR!!
Hey, no fair!

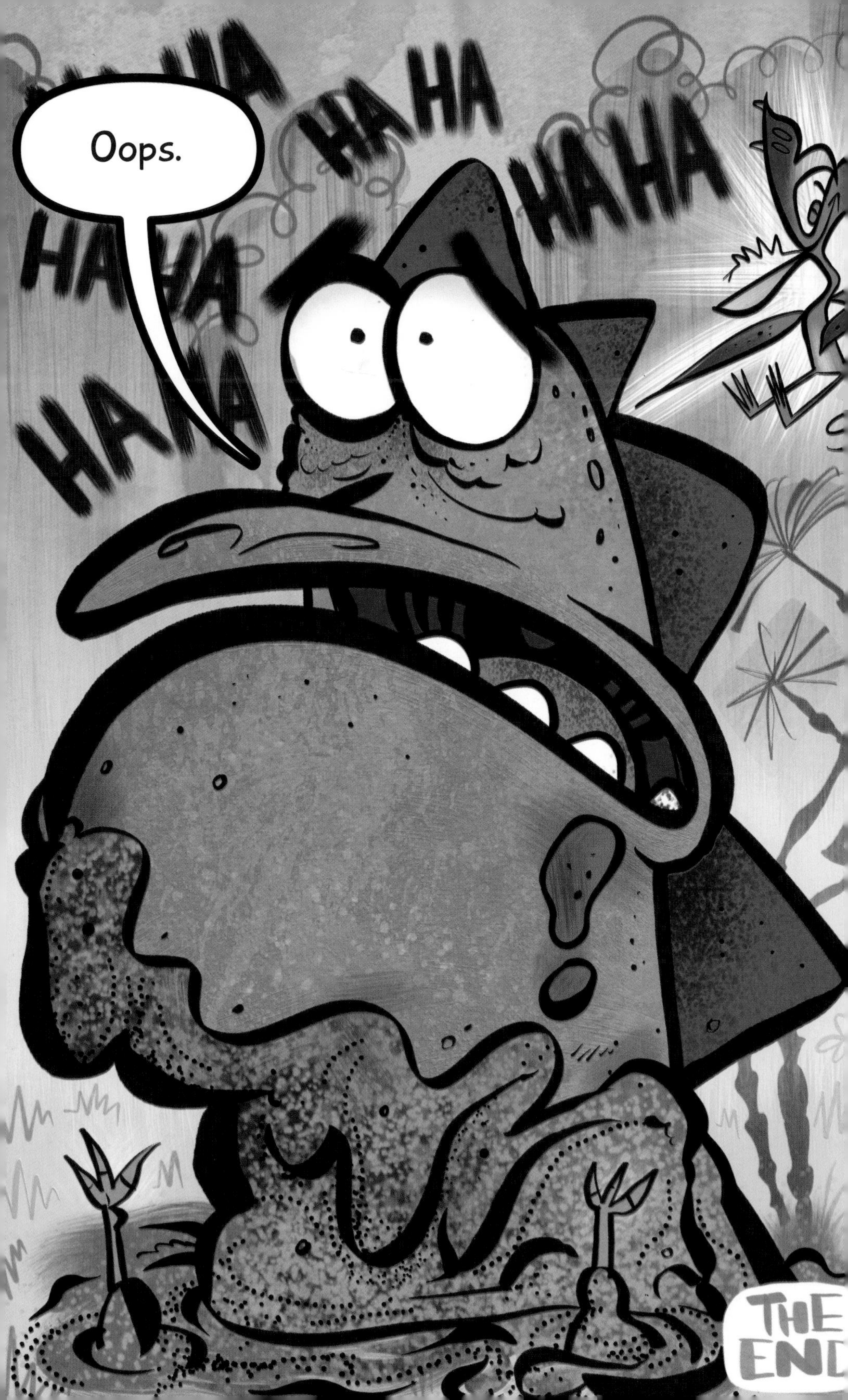
HA HA
HA HA
HAHA
HAHA
HAHA
Oops.
THE END